THE 1950s SPANKING CHRONICLES

TRUE SPANKING STORIES FROM THE FIFTIES

VOLUME I

THE 1950s SPANKING CHRONICLES

TRUE SPANKING STORIES FROM THE FIFTIES

VOLUME I

True accounts from the Nineteen–Fifties, the Golden Age of Spanking: erotic spanking, discipline spanking, punishment spanking, corporal punishment, domestic discipline, OTK spanking, BDSM spanking, kinky spanking and spanking fetishism, with hand, hairbrush, paddle, strap, switch and more.

Edited by
SASHA CAVE

Nelson & Jones

THE 1950s SPANKING CHRONICLES: TRUE SPANKING STORIES FROM THE FIFTIES, VOLUME I: True accounts from the Nineteen–Fifties, the Golden Age of Spanking: erotic spanking, discipline spanking, punishment spanking, corporal punishment, domestic discipline, OTK spanking, BDSM spanking, kinky spanking and spanking fetishism, with hand, hairbrush, paddle, strap, switch and more.

Edited by Sasha Cave

Nelson & Jones
2272 Colorado Boulevard, #100
Los Angeles, California 90041
www.SpankingBible.com

Publisher's Cataloguing–in–Publication Data
Cave, Sasha, Editor.
THE 1950s SPANKING CHRONICLES: TRUE SPANKING STORIES FROM THE FIFTIES, VOLUME I: True accounts from the Nineteen–Fifties, the Golden Age of Spanking: erotic spanking, discipline spanking, punishment spanking, corporal punishment, domestic discipline, OTK spanking, BDSM spanking, kinky spanking and spanking fetishism, with hand, hairbrush, paddle, strap, switch and more./ Sasha Cave, editor – 1st edition
    p. cm.
ISBN 13:   978-0-918898-35-7 (paperback)
ISBN 10:   0-918898-35-8
    1. American erotic literature. I. Title.
Library of Congress Control Number: 2011908893

TABLE OF CONTENTS

FOREWORD

PLEASE JOIN OUR MAILING LIST

Please add your name to our Email list to receive information on future books and spanking–related news and special offers. Just visit www.SpankingBible.com and click on the link.

PLEASE SEND US YOUR SPANKING EXPERIENCE

Do you have an interesting spanking experience? We would be delighted to review it for possible publication in a future volume of this series. Just visit www.SpankingBible.com and click on the Email link.

PLEASE GIVE US YOUR COMMENTS ON THIS BOOK

We would appreciate your comments on this book. What did you like? Why? Not like? Why? Which true story was your favorite? Any suggestions for future books like this? We'd love to hear from you! Please visit www.SpankingBible.com and click on the Email link.

PLEASE POST FIVE–STAR REVIEWS AND RATINGS ON AMAZON.COM AND OTHER SITES

Please post five–star reviews and ratings on Amazon.com and other sites, so other people can enjoy this book. Thank you.

EDITOR'S INTRODUCTION

The nineteen–fifties have been called "The Golden Age of Spanking." The true 1950s spanking accounts in this book are not only exciting and erotic in themselves; they open a window into a fascinating era. You are privileged to take part in a groundbreaking publishing event; except for museum curators and a few dedicated collectors, few people have seen most of this material for more than fifty years.

This book is largely drawn from the many spanking letters and articles that appeared in '50s magazines — magazines for men, women, and in a few cases teenage girls. The contributors vividly describe their many spanking experiences and relationships:

Parents and other relatives spanking teenagers;

Brothers, sisters and cousins spanking each other, either because one was put in authority over another, or for erotic experimentation in adolescence;

Spankings in high school, typically but not always with the paddle;

Spankings in college. Paddling was universal in sorority initiations. And many a coed who turned in poor work risked having a professor or teaching assistant put her over their knees for motivation.

Spankings in reformatories;

Spankings by police, who often dispensed informal punishment with a handy strap or paddle, with full parental approval;

Employers spanking young women employees, apparently a surprisingly common practice;

Boyfriends spanking girlfriends and husbands spanking wives, and vice–versa, both for discipline and sexual pleasure;

And much, much more.

Strikingly, the experiences in this book aren't just from men's magazines, but from many types of publications. Newspapers and mainstream magazines had frequent spanking letters, articles and advice. Letters about whether teenagers or wives should be spanked, often with details about how they *were* spanked, even graced *Life* and *Look*. Perhaps most surprisingly, many spanking letters appeared in magazines for teenage girls and young women, such as *My Romance*. Spanking of all sorts also permeated advertising, movies and TV.

The vivid experiences in this book remind us that spanking was everywhere in the '50's. Most high schools used the paddle, or (more rarely) yardstick, strap, cane or switch. The same implements met bare bottoms by the thousands in boys' and girls' reformatories. Many a police car carried a paddle or strap in the trunk to deal with vandalism, curfew violations and other petty mischief.

All the spanking outside the home reflected behavior inside the home, with many experiences described here. Most parents spanked their children for bad behavior, often through adolescence. Even young adult women were often spanked if they remained under their parents' roof. Many men spanked their wives, and a surprising number were spanked by their wives.

Considering the erotic implications of spanking, no wonder young men and women reacted to the thought or even the word "spanking." For them it was an excuse to do to their girlfriend what their dad did to their sister, or even to their mother. The very thought of wrestling a squirming, squealing, insincerely protesting girl across their knee, baring as much as they could get away with, and spanking a girlish bottom till it was hot and flushed, excited a whole generation of boys. And the girls along with the boys.

There were as many types of spanking in the '50s as there are today, and this book shows all. At one pole the spankings are frankly sexual, where "pain is the path to pleasure." At the opposite pole are disciplinary spankings, where pain tangles with emotions like submission and humiliation, but may yet morph into pleasure.

In between these poles you will find every sort of spanking, with every purpose, feeling, emotion and result. And in every relationship and situation: husband/wife, boyfriend/girlfriend, girlfriend/girlfriend, parent/adolescent, brother/sister, teacher or principal/student, professor/coed, sorority sister/pledge, employer/secretary and more. Plus punishments where those in trouble must submit to authority: police and teenage delinquents; jailers and their charges in reformatories and prisons; military police and prisoners in the brig.

Within these pages are spankings as domestic discipline. And in power exchange relationships of dominance–submission or sado–masochism, where spanking may be spiced with other edgy activities such as clothes fetishism, bondage, medical play, age play and anal play. Yes, even in the '50s.

"Spanking" in this book's title stands for every implement, position and technique. Merely skimming the book, one finds in action the strap, tailed strap, belt, slipper, hairbrush, paddle (short and long, light and heavy, solid or holed), cane, switch, riding crop, ruler, yardstick, and many more. And last but certainly not least, the firm hand, vigorously applied to bouncing buttocks.

Every position is here. Every technique, detail and ritual. Few spanks or many. Slow–paced or fast. Corner time. Spanking in front of others. Spanking combined with other punishments. *Of course*, spanking combined with sex.

Every emotion and feeling appears, and often many emotions tangled together: pain; pain with pleasure; submission with self–realization, security and love. And, of course, sexual excitement and release, all the more powerful because sexuality was suppressed in the '50s and spanking allowed its release.

Be warned that this book includes experiences of dominance and submission, erotic embarrassment, bondage, non–consensual spanking, other punishment, exhibitionism and voyeurism, homoerotic relationships, anal eroticism and various kinds of sex.

I have tried to show as broad a range of spanking experiences as I could. However, I favored the most exciting and vivid accounts, and those revealing not just the spankings' details but physical and emotional feelings. Last names of people and some names of places, companies, organizations and colleges have been removed for privacy or legal reasons. Titles of letters are mostly added only for the reader's convenience.

Otherwise, though, the writers speak directly to you from 50 years ago as intimately as if you were there, watching them spank and be spanked. I hope you enjoy reading these experiences as much as I enjoyed choosing the best ones for you.

— Sasha Cave, Editor

THE 1950S SPANKING CHRONICLES:

TRUE SPANKING STORIES FROM THE FIFTIES

VOLUME I

"MOST WOMEN ARE WILLING"

— ALBERT W., CALIFORNIA

I have always enjoyed spanking a well–rounded, firm female bottom. I don't mean whipping or blood letting. I am not cruel, not a sadist. But during a six year period of my young single life, I made an effort to try to spank as many "nice girls" as I could. I played my cards carefully and patiently and tried to use the best strategy and tactics with each girl, reading her like a poker opponent.

In most cases I reached my goal. When the young women were convinced that I wasn't a crazy and would not take advantage of them sexually — unless I already was! — most were quite willing to crawl over my lap for reasonable punishment, with the understanding that they could stop it if necessary.

Out of fifty one girls, only eleven refused to be spanked. The others allowed me to spank their bare bottoms until the skin was hot and bright pink, almost red. Some allowed me to go much farther. Most of the 40 willing ones allowed many more spankings, showing they enjoyed the experience. In the additional spankings, they would typically allow me to punish them more severely. But I never punished a girl to the point of bruises or blood blisters; they were always almost "good as new" in a day or two.

Certainly there was nothing sadistic or cruel about the spankings, and the girls weren't hardcore masochists; just healthy, curious young women willing to try something new. When I see any of these women, they remember the spankings warmly.

I am now married to a very pretty young wife who enjoys at least two spankings a week almost as much as I enjoy giving them. In fact, she is usually the one who thinks up scenes and roles to make the event even more exciting. For example, she often puts on high school clothes of the sort worn when we were both that age. Then she acts like a rebellious, naughty girl who has disobeyed her parents and gotten caught.

I enjoy myself lecturing my bratty teenage "daughter." Then I lower her poodle skirt and panties, place her over my knee and spank her perfect bottom until she cries loudly and promises to behave and do whatever I tell her. After this spanking role–play we are both eager for sex.

There is no reason to judge old–fashioned spankings as sadistic. In addition to the sexy spankings I give my wife, spankings are an effective means of discipline. My mother spanked my two sisters and me until we were past our middle teens. She wasn't a sadist and she wasn't brutal. She simply believed in the power of a strap, applied to a bare teenage backside, to change problem behavior. We didn't develop an abnormal need for bare–bottomed discipline; the spankings we got satisfied any curiosity we might have had.

Spankings were a common means of discipline then; most of my friends in junior high and high school got the strap, paddle or hairbrush at least occasionally. I remember one time a girl I knew opened her report card. When she saw her bad grades, her face fell and her hand went involuntarily to her cute backside. A real tip–off!

My two sisters get paddled by their husbands, but, like my marriage, it is for pleasure and foreplay before sex, not sadistic punishment.

x x x

"SHE LIVES TO BE PUT ACROSS THEIR KNEE"

— MRS. H. Y., OMAHA, NEBRASKA

I am one of probably many women (and men) who get pleasure through *mild* giving and getting pain. I am 34, clean–living, non–smoking, non–drinking, politically conservative. No one would assume I have unusual interests. But I live for the times when someone, either man or woman, puts me across the knee and spanks me soundly. In turn, I enjoy spanking someone else's bottom, whether they be man or woman.

I am not interested in brutality. Brutal lashings or beatings are of no interest, in fact they turn me off. But a good spanking, over the knee with hairbrush, paddle, table tennis bat, sawed off bathbrush, or just a firm hand, is wonderful. I feel 100 % better every time I get one, or give one. Or, ideally, exchange spankings.

I don't know the connection between desires like mine and childhood experiences. I have met spanking enthusiasts (both spankers and spanked) who were spanked in childhood and as teens; I have met others with no interest in spanking who were similarly punished. On the other hand, I know many people who were never spanked as children and teens, and some enjoy spanking as adults while others don't. I'll let the experts argue about all that.

In my case, I remember with pleasure and excitement the

spankings my father gave me in my teens. I have to say he enjoyed it, since he made a ceremony out of each time. He would take me in a room alone. I was never punished in front of siblings, or I might have different feelings entirely. He'd sit on a chair while I stood in front of him, and lecture me on why I was going to be punished. Usually I wanted him to just cut it short and go ahead and blister me and get it done with.

Then he took me across his lap. He would apply his palm to my seat at a steady pace. It hurt, yet I enjoyed the stinging and warmth in my bottom. Very rarely, he would use a small paddle, and that hurt a lot more but I still enjoyed it. Adults who enjoy being spanked will understand these conflicting feelings. Even more rarely, my clothing and panties would come down, and then the pain, the stinging and warmth and the embarrassment all got mixed up together.

In college, as a freshman, I was often spanked by a senior who obviously enjoyed it a lot. There are many men and women who love to be paddled. There are many others who love doing the paddling. There are plenty who enjoy crossing over regularly or at least sometimes.

I know many people complain that it's hard to find a partner, either to be spanked or to spank them. I don't buy that. I have learned to always be alert to an interest in spanking when I meet new people. There are telltale clues in conversation, and you can steer the conversation to movies or books that include spanking, or a scandal where the reports mentioned spanking, or theories of child raising or dealing with juvenile delinquents, or reminiscences of adolescent mischief and punishment, or . . .

In short, with careful probing, it is possible to find spanking partners without too much difficulty. That has been my experience in college, in major cities including Chicago, Los Angeles, Omaha, Nebraska and Paris, France, and in small U.S. towns as well. I have never even resorted to running advertisements, another way to troll for partners.

The spanking partners I have found, and there have been dozens, have not been perverted, unhappy or twisted. They have just enjoyed either giving or receiving spankings. Sometimes we had a sexual relationship as well, sometimes not. Most people who regularly get spankings enjoy them and find them exciting, enjoyable, often sexually gratifying and relaxing.

I do think that if a woman has a strong interest in spanking, she should discuss it with her prospective partner before getting married. If the man has a strong aversion to spanking, they are headed for friction. On the other hand, even if the man has no interest in spanking, the relationship can thrive if he enters fully into the spirit of the [spanko's] desires, and gives the frequent paddlings the woman wants. Spankings in marriage aren't cruelty, they are pleasuring that involves physical, emotional and sexual feelings.

Those who mock spanking enthusiasts don't know what they're missing and should try it sometime. Those of us who enjoy these sessions wouldn't dream of giving them up.

x x x

EMBARRASSING PUNISHMENT DOES WONDERS FOR HIS DAUGHTERS

— ROBERT Q., MICHIGAN

Agree with with you that [extreme sadism] is a dangerous thing. However, I firmly believe in reasonable corporal punishment for sons and daughters and I feel this is a very different thing from sadism.

To take my own case, I have daughters aged sixteen and fourteen. The older one is a fine young woman and the younger one nearly there, because I have always kept an old hairbrush close at hand and reached for it without hesitation when my daughters' conduct required its use. Even today, I am ready to put either one over my knee for a good long panties–down spanking.

I do not spank unreasonably hard. However, every hairbrush spanking ends with the young woman having a scarlet rear end and crying uncontrollably. My daughters find these bare bottom spankings both very painful and very embarrassing.

However, they do seem to work wonders. Both girls agree this is the most effective way to keep them on the straight path. Evidently they do have a good effect as the need for them has become rarer and rarer as the girls matured.

I know that my two brothers spank their own teenage daughters the same as I do, except that one uses only his hand rather than a hairbrush. However, he's a bricklayer, with very strong

6

hands, so I doubt his daughter gets off easy. I suspect there are millions of teenage girls and boys who regularly know the pain of a hand, hairbrush or strap across their bare bottoms. I know that some of my friends spank their teenage children, since we sometimes talk about child raising and give each other advice. Also, my daughters see other girls in the school locker room and group showers, and sometimes it is obvious a girl has been spanked.

When I spank I am always in a calm frame of mind. I simply smack my daughter's behind until it reaches the desired red hue and state of pain, and she reaches the desired attitude of contrition. Although her bottom may be deeply red and mottled, I stop far short of bruises or any harm. Also, we do not hold grudges. When she stops crying, I help her up and give her a hug.

I'm crazy about my wonderful daughters and would never do anything cruel to them. This is just fatherly love and necessary discipline.

x x x

SPANKED BY HER PROFESSOR

— KATHY M., UNIVERSITY PARK, PENNSYLVANIA

I am a young woman of 19 who enjoys a spanking. I believe this interest in getting spanked is widely shared, and by more women than men.

I have been fascinated by spanking since my early teens. Having studied the subject, including psychology, anatomy and physiology, I'd like to point out some interesting facts about spanking and the female body. It is clear that the female bottom is an extremely sensitive erotic zone and gives the woman sexual pleasure when it is stroked, patted, squeezed or stimulated in any way. So there is nothing "abnormal" in a woman's physical or psychological development when she enjoys having her bottom smacked.

Women differ in their physical and psychological. So arguments about whether women should be spanked "lightly" or "reasonably" or "severely" are almost pointless. Women's responses to spanking fall along a spectrum or distributional "bell curve." While some women would agree that a particular spanking is light, moderate or severe, other women crave and respond to spankings that their sisters could not tolerate.

Some of your writers speculate that a wish to be spanked may result from childhood associations, such as being spanked by a parent or beloved older sibling. That may be true for some, but my own case suggests otherwise.

I was never spanked by either of my parents when growing up. Nor by a sibling, uncle, or other relative. Nor at school. I wasn't even spanked at my birthday parties. My bottom was first warmed when I joined the girl's basketball team in high school. I was almost 15.

As part of the initiation, each of the older members gave the new girls a swat with a wooden paddle, while we bent over and held our ankles. We did get to wear panties. However, the paddlers pulled the new girls' panties into their bottom cleft, so we were decent, but our poor bottom cheeks had zero protection. Those swats stung an awful lot and left us new girls bright red and burning.

All of us new girls suffered from this paddling, and all of us, including me, cried, but I enjoyed it despite the pain. It was unbearably exciting and I kept reliving the pain and my mental feelings afterward, especially late at night.

By the way, the school knew about this initiation. In fact, the team captain borrowed the paddle from the team coach, who only warned her not to "go easy" on us. All the sports teams, boys and girls, had similar initiations. The school thought they built team spirit. All the parents knew about the initiations too, but shrugged.

After that paddling, I often longed for a hard, old–fashioned, over the knee paddling. (But I would have settled for bending over and getting the strap, paddle, switch or the cane that they used to use on schoolboys in England.) I envied my girlfriends and their brothers and sisters who got spanked over the knee regularly for misbehavior. But I didn't see that I could ask their parents to spank me as a favor, and if I had approached mine they would have sent me to a therapist. In the meantime the closest I could come was an occasional playful bottom swat from boyfriends. Again, if I had asked for a "real" spanking, I would have gotten a strange reputation. I must say, though, that I enjoyed subsequent team initiations where I was among those wielding the paddle on the backsides of cute new members.

It wasn't until my freshman year in college that I got my first "real" spanking.

I figured out how to get it. While discussing old English literature, the professor had made a few comments and jokes about corporal punishment; about how maids were spanked or birched by their lords and ladies, and children and teens were punished by their governesses and tutors. These asides, along with the professor being English, were enough of a hint. After doing excellent work, I purposely turned in an awful paper so that the prof would call me to his office for a talk.

Instead of being contrite, I acted sullen and bratty. I was overjoyed when he said I was spoiled and had a bad attitude and joked that I "needed a good spanking like tutors would give pupils in the old days." To his amazement, I agreed that he was right, and asked if I could get a spanking (and re-edit the paper) instead of getting a bad grade.

He was reluctant at first, since any "sexual" contact with students violated college rules. I had to promise over and over that I wouldn't tell a soul, and beg him to go ahead and "be a man" about it. Finally I won him over and he ordered me over his knee. I eagerly did so before he could change his mind.

He began spanking me with his hand on the back of my skirt, but I hardly felt it. He asked me if I was learning my lesson, and I laughed and said, "No." Just as I'd hoped, he pulled my skirt up and started spanking me on my panties. That really stung, but when he asked whether I was feeling it now, I laughed again. At last — *finally!* — he pulled my panties down to my knees and really started stinging my bare bottom, and it felt wonderful. I was getting what I had needed for years.

He spanked me hard and long. I never asked him to stop, just cried and squirmed around. I was in Seventh Heaven. He stopped only for fear he might be damaging my precious bottom.

After that, the professor spanked me regularly, and I loved it every time. I didn't have to turn in bad work to give him an excuse. We'd simply get together and enjoy ourselves. He was married and we never did anything sexual. The closest we came was that he'd rub my behind after the spanking and tell me how hot it felt and what a pretty girl I was. But he'd never even put his finger in me or touch my sexual parts. I'd have been more than willing. On the other hand, with all the squirming back and forth over his knees . . .

I have thought a lot about what triggers an interest in being spanked. I don't think it comes from childhood punishment. I know many girls who were spanked in childhood, and many who were not. I can't find a correlation with whether they enjoy spanking now or not.

I think that, whether or not there was previous spanking, there is usually a formative or trigger spanking experience *just as the woman's mind and body are awakening sexually.* (My own trigger at 15 happened rather late.) The erotic physical, mental and emotional sensations are so powerful that even a single incident can make spanking erotically charged for the woman. Perhaps that's what happened to me at the paddling initiation back in high school.

I hope my personal reminiscences are interesting and useful. I believe the best scholarly investigation comes from actual experience. Don't you agree?

X X X

TEEN SUFFERS UNFAIR SPANKINGS FROM HER BROTHER–IN–LAW

— SARAH F., NORTH READING, MASSACHUSETTS

I am a 16–year–old girl. After my parents died, I have lived with my older sister and her husband, both 26. The recent letters about spanking help explain some things I had been wondering about.

I have lived with my sister and her husband for four years. Before that, I got spanked by both my parents, but not very often, and not so hard, or in the same way as my sister and brother–in–law spank me. What I am driving at is that I think my sister and brother–in–law *enjoy* spanking me, and I don't think this is right.

Why do I say this? For one thing, because I get spanked so often although I am very well–behaved both at home and outside home. For another, because they make such a ritual out of it. For another, because whenever I get punished, they *both* punish me, watching each other, and I think they both get kind of *excited* by the spanking.

They have an elaborate system of different levels of spanking depending on what I did wrong. For example, getting bad grades means a hand spanking of 12 hard spanks from each of them. I have to take off my dress or raise my skirt up, but am allowed to keep my panties on for modesty.

12

For being out past their curfew, it's also over the knee but they don't use their hands. They use tools instead. They have a large flat oak hairbrush used only for spanking. They also have a ping pong paddle; the kind with a hard rubber pebbled surface.

Usually they make me choose whether I want to be spanked with the hairbrush or the ping pong paddle. The number of spanks depends on how late I was. Up to ten minutes late, I get the regular dose of 12 from each. Over that, I get one more from each for every three minutes or fraction of a minute I'm late. For example, recently I was late 20 minutes. So I got 12 + 4 from each. That's 12 for the first 10 minutes late, and 4 for the next 10 minutes.

For the worst faults, they take everything down and punish my bare bottom. Back talking means 16 hand spanks from each on the bare. Swearing or using the Lord's name means getting one of the correction tools from each on the bare.

I am required to cooperate with the spanking and maintain a good attitude even while being spanked. If I protest, try to escape, or complain or wiggle around during the spanking, I get much worse. For example, even if I am due for a hand spanking, I may get more spanks, get them on the bare, or they may decide to use the ping pong paddle or hairbrush on the bare.

That happened recently. I was being spanked by hand for coming back only minutes late. I was over my brother–in–law's knee and he and my sister were teasing me before he actually started. I got upset and said something I shouldn't have. My sister bared my bottom completely and then they really teased me. My brother–in–law gave me a really hard hand spanking. Even though I was already crying and apologizing, he made me choose a spanking tool.

I didn't want to, but he said, "Choose one or you'll get both." I didn't want that, so I chose the paddle. He gave me a whole lot of hard smacks with that. Meanwhile my sister stood behind me laughing and teasing me and telling him spots he'd missed. After all that, he turned me over to her and she repeated my dose, not a single spank less.

As for enjoying spankings, no thank you. I think a very mild spanking from someone you love, when they are sincerely doing it for your own good (like with my parents when I was younger) can be a special experience. It sort of feels interesting, and the warmth and sting afterward is okay too.

But the spankings from my sister and brother–in–law are different. They are very painful, and the pain lasts for a long time if they have used the paddle or hairbrush. Also I feel very embarrassed with my brother–in–law, especially when they bare me. I am totally ashamed and I don't think it's right to bare me like that. I also don't think it helps my behavior very much. I am sure they spank me for their own enjoyment. They like to joke, "This hurts me more than it hurts you," but that's not true. It hurts *me* an awful lot, embarrasses *me* horribly, but *they* enjoy it.

They have so many rules and the rules are so complicated that they find a chance to spank me at least twice a week. It seems like the moment I'm back to my normal color and not hurting anymore, they look for an excuse to get me over the lap again.

They've also threatened me with other punishments, like washing my mouth out with soap or imposing "punishment enemas." They've never done those things, but the threat keeps me scared and makes me cooperate "eagerly" with the spankings.

My brother–in–law spanks my sister, too, but I don't know the details. I've never been invited to watch, but I can hear the sounds from their bedroom.

I feel trapped. I have no money, nowhere to live and no way to support myself. I tried to talk to a teacher I like at school, but she said my sister and brother–in–law are taking my parents' place so they have the right to spank me. She didn't want to hear the details. So I guess I'm in for years of spankings.

I'm sorry I can't give my full name.

x x x

IS IT "SEXUAL" TO SPANK?

— JANET I., TAOS, NEW MEXICO

'd like to present my own view [on the spanking controversy]. Until I married (at 17, underage but with parents' consent), my parents spanked me, or to be more exact strapped me, for serious misbehavior. They didn't have to spank me very often; it hurt so much that one session lasted me for quite awhile. After my 13th birthday, I'd guess I was spanked about 4 times a year. Spankings were always given on my bare buttocks. They wetted them first, then I got dad's razor strop until they felt the lesson had taken. I was in pain for a long time afterward, too, and my buttocks didn't return to normal color for even longer.

My sister and brother were treated the same way, and I am positive no sexual reason was involved with my strappings or theirs. My parents were very loving, decent people and these strappings were ordinary measures of child discipline, fair and *very* effective. After a strapping I'd think three times before getting out of line anytime soon.

One thing I liked was that after the *strapping* was over, I knew the *punishment* was over. My parents would hug me and assure me of their love, and how they hated having to punish me like that, etc. I would tell them I loved them too and apologize for my conduct. With that, the matter was closed and the slate wiped clean. There were no angry words, no arguments, no scolding.

I admit I deserved every strapping I got, except one when I

was 15 and was wrongly blamed for vandalism another girl had done. When the truth came out later, my parents felt awful about punishing me. I felt awful because they hadn't believed me.

I am now married and have two wonderful teenage daughters of my own. My husband and I are raising them with the same philosophy as my parents. (His parents were no model for anything.) Our girls say they are lucky we punish them in this way. Most of their friends' parents deprive their children of privileges, ground them and so on rather than punish them physically. Their friends say that breeds resentment and constant arguments.

Our daughters' friends say my daughters are lucky to be spanked. Getting grounded cheats them of activities such as school football games and dances, concerts and excursions they may have looked forward to for weeks. Thus the girls are not only bitterly disappointed as the event approaches, but deprived of their interaction with their friends. Also, they are embarrassed because everyone realizes by their absence they have been punished.

My husband has the same philosophy with me that we have with our daughters. He will take me over his knee when I need it, and a good spanking works the same wonders with me now as it did when I was my daughters' age. I get spanked rarely — perhaps once every three months. My spankings are bare buttocks, the same as our daughters.' I get spanked only for serious misbehavior or attitude, just as with our daughters. My husband uses his hand, then a hairbrush.

There is nothing sexual about either the spankings our daughters get, or mine. I am sure of this for many reasons:

1. My parents and my husband all tried everything they could do to avoid having to spank me. Spanking was always a last resort, not a first resort. If they'd been getting sexual gratification out of spanking me, they'd have been looking for excuses to punish me more often.

2. On the other side of the coin, I am not masochistic. Both as a teenager and now I do everything I can to avoid a spanking; they *hurt* too much. The only thing worse than being bent over

my husband's knee getting the hairbrush, is being bent over our bed or a convenient piece of furniture getting the razor strop on my bare buttocks. It's both agonizingly painful and very embarrassing. If I got sexually excited by being punished like this, I'd be trying to get punished more. I don't! I do admire and respect my husband for being firm and keeping me in line, like my dad used to.

3. My husband does everything he can to avoid having to spank the girls (and so do I). I usually have to insist they need a spanking. He'd rather let close calls slide and let them get away with a talking–to or something trivial like extra chores. If my husband were sadistic, he'd be eager to spank them frequently, especially since they are both beautiful girls.

4. My daughters absolutely do not like being spanked. No more than I did at their ages! Usually a spanking ends that particular misbehavior for quite some time. Again, if they were getting sexual gratification from being spanked, they would repeat, rather than avoid, the misbehavior.

My husband and I are both college graduates, and he has a master's and doctorate as well. We're both from Colorado, although we live in New Mexico. He works as an executive in an electrical engineering firm. I am a homemaker and also teach violin part time. Our girls are 14 and 15.

My sister and brother are happily married and also employ corporal punishment with their children. My sister also gets spanked by her husband. He didn't want to at first; but she insisted it was good for her and eventually converted him.

Interestingly, my brother does not spank his wife. *She* was willing; *he* is the one who doesn't want to. Go figure.

Our method of administering punishment to our daughters is the same as when I was a girl. First we listen to the girl's explanation; sometimes we accept it as reasonable and there is no punishment. Otherwise, we send her to her room to await punishment. My husband and I discuss the matter, and if we agree that spanking is needed, we summon her.

After we are sure our daughter understands why she deserves severe punishment, my husband orders our daughter to come to him. She raises her dress and I use a pin or clothespins to hold it above her waist. Then I pull her panties down to her ankles. My husband arranges her in a comfortable position, bent over the sofa arm with her nude buttocks prominently displayed.

Then my husband uses the razor strop hard and long on our daughter's bare buttocks, especially the lower part, and the top of her thighs just below her buttocks. I decide when to stop. I stop when she is reduced to a blubbering little girl, with her buttocks striped red and deep red, and her whole body shaking. A teenage girl is not a small child. She has to be *well–spanked* for the spanking to do her good. That means helplessly crying and honestly repentant. I know from experience!

Occasionally, when my husband is away and one of the girls needs punishment, I will spank her. I do it over my knee, bottom bare of course, and use a hairbrush to assist my strong right arm. I'm not as strong as my husband, but I try to make up for it by spanking many more times. As with the strop, my goal is to reduce the misbehaving child to a state of pain, crying and repentance.

We don't count the number of spanks, either with the strop or hairbrush. It varies with the seriousness of the misbehavior. I pride myself on judging when the punishment has been sufficient, judging from buttocks color, crying and the girl's statements and attitude.

When the spanking is over, the dress is unpinned and the girl is allowed to put herself in order. When she regains her composure (no longer crying, breathing normally) she rejoins the family. He misbehavior is put in the past and we don't mention it or the spanking again. Our children are not allowed to tease each other about being spanked, on pain of getting what their sister got.

Our daughters are not punished in front of each other, even when they have misbehaved together. The strapping or hairbrush spanking is painful and embarrassing enough without their sister watching.

Our girls say that about a fourth of the girls they know get spanked, at least occasionally for serious misbehavior; the others get punished with groundings and loss of privileges. Most of their friends would prefer spankings to the punishments they get. Though our daughters find their spankings painful, they much prefer them to other punishments like most of their friends get.

SPANKED WITH HIS UNCLE'S YARDSTICK

— RONNIE S., DAVID CITY, NEBRASKA

I am a man of eighteen and a college freshman. I am the only child of middle class parents, both of whom are college graduates, well established in good jobs. Growing up, I was never physically punished.

Just before I finished high school last June, at the age of seventeen, an uncle living in Oklahoma asked me if I would like to live with him during the summer and earn some money for college. He was able to get me an excellent job that was almost full time, unlike my own town, where work was scarce and poorly paid. My parents gave their whole–hearted approval, and a week after graduation I stepped off the Greyhound.

My uncle is my mother's little brother. He's thirty years old, a college graduate, and employed in a very highly–paid, low–work government job. He's a bachelor, charming and strikingly handsome. With these advantages, along with plenty of money and a cushy job that leaves him ample leisure, he is very popular with women.

After dinner a few days after I arrived, my uncle casually mentioned that he knew I had never been physically disciplined at home. Since I was living in his house, it was reasonable for his house rules to apply, I wasn't too old for a spanking, and I could expect corporal punishment if I got out of line. We both laughed. I wasn't even sure if he was serious, and I thought nothing more of it. I should have thought about it, though.

That Friday, my uncle asked that I do certain chores around the house over the weekend. I was having so much fun with my new friends from work, however, that I let it slide. That Sunday evening he observed to me that none of the chores had been touched. He wasn't angry and said he'd like me to find time to do them during the week.

However, he reminded me of his previous warning about spanking, and said I would have to be punished to help me remember to do things as promised next time. He told me to go to my room. I was uncertain and nervous about what was going to happen.

My uncle knew I had been planning to go out that evening. When he came to my room, he was carrying a wooden yardstick. He said he wasn't going to keep me from going out, and we had plenty of time "to get our little punishment out of the way." He talked to me a few minutes about how important it was to fulfill my commitments. Then he told me to lie face down on the bed.

I was both scared and excited. I was scared because of the pain I expected. Like I said, I had never been spanked, not with a hand or anything else, and that yardstick looked serious. It was the curiosity which made me do what he ordered. That, plus the fact I knew he could make me do what he wanted if I didn't co-operate. So I got on the bed, over two pillows which raised my buttocks up. He made me pull down my pants but let me keep my underwear on.

Then he began to spank my buttocks with his hand. After he did this about ten times hard on each side, he started spanking me with the yardstick.

He spanked me with the yardstick many times for about five minutes, and the pain was so bad I had to grit my teeth, but still ended up crying. When he finally finished, he said he thought the spanking did me some good. I was in pain for about fifteen minutes, but after that the stinging gradually went away, leaving only warmth as a reminder. I realized my spanking had been a mixture of pain and excitement, and it wasn't that bad all in all. Still, I tried to stay out of trouble.

However, two weeks later, I stayed after work to socialize

with my buddies, and lost track of the time. When I got home, well past our dinnertime, my father was dining alone and my food was cold. I apologized for being late and not calling. My uncle said it was okay.

My uncle was pleasant enough during dinner, but after dinner he asked me whether I had earned a punishment for coming home late without calling. Being in two minds, I mad a show of trying to get out of punishment, but said, he was right and I understood.

Once again I heard the fatal words, "Please go to your room." My uncle came in behind me, and again he was carrying the yardstick. He told me to drop my pants and underwear and lean over a footstool in the room. I realized he intended to spank my bare buttocks, and I became both frightened and excited. He hit me at least thirty times with the yardstick. It was much worse on the bare, and this time I bawled like a baby. When he finished, he told me to stay in position five minutes and think about why I'd been punished. Then he said I'd taken my spanking well.

When I looked at my buttocks in the mirror afterward, there were red stripes across both cheeks, one on top of another. This time there wasn't any warm afterglow any time soon; they hurt all night.

For the rest of the summer, my uncle spanked me about every week and a half, always on my bare buttocks. In addition to the yardstick, several times he made me cut a switch from the backyard and used that on my lower buttocks and upper thighs. In case you've never been switched, it burns! It's like a line of bee stings right across your buttocks. Also, sometimes the switch, being flexible, comes around and gets you on the side of your legs, which is even worse than on the buttocks.

I still don't know whether my uncle enjoyed spanking me or not. I assume so, or he wouldn't have done it so much. Every spanking was very painful, but by the end of the summer I'd been totally hooked; I loved being spanked. I suppose the spankings also made me more reliable and considerate, too.

x x x

SCHOOLHOUSE WHIPPINGS

— SAMANTHA L., ANDOVER, MASSACHUSETTS

At one time I wouldn't have dreamed I could enjoy being spanked or spanking anyone else. Now I know better.

As a girl I was well–loved and well–spanked. My parents were quite strict. Bad behavior meant a sound correction, and the correction was on my bare buttocks. I was spanked by both parents, whichever one happened to be around or less busy when I misbehaved or they learned about it. They used only their hand, but that was more than enough to get the lesson across.

The schools I went to paddled students, but I was well–behaved at school and never got it.

Up until my teens I got no joy out of being spanked by my parents; just pain. And, as I grew older and more body conscious, embarrassment, especially when my father did the spanking. However, by thirteen I began to get excited when I was going to be spanked. I greatly enjoyed my spankings, although at my innocent age I didn't make the connection about the sexual feelings I was getting until I was almost fifteen.

At twenty three I got a job teaching at a one room "little red schoolhouse" in the "hills and hollers" [literally, "hollows" or valleys — Ed.] of Tennessee. On the day I was hired, the head of the School Board for the district told me, "If they don't behave, whip 'em. The kids won't refuse and their parents will back you up. If the kid refuses, write the parents. They'll give the kid worse, then bring 'em in for *your* whipping."

I tried to hide my amazement at this advice. I needed to ask, "What do I whip 'em with? How hard? With their britches on or off?" But I wanted to sound competent, like I had "whipped" kids a thousand times and this was routine.

Kids will always test a new teacher's limits, and soon enough I found brats that required punishment. One fourteen–year–old boy baited me until, despite my nerves, I decided I had to act. I ordered him to stay after school.

With no discussion, I ordered, "Drop 'em now. You're getting spanked."

To my surprise, he obeyed without hesitation. Then I ordered, "Your underpants too. What makes you think you deserve protection?"

He hesitated, and blushed, but those came down too.

Although he was far bigger than me, I put him over my knee and spanked him with my hand as hard as I could. There's nothing like jumping into the water. As soon as I started spanking him my nerves went away and were replaced by excitement, satisfaction and pleasure. Long before his quivering cheeks reached the desired shade of dark red, he was crying and begging me to stop. I ignored his pleas. He squirmed in pain and discomfort, but I told him to stay still or the spanking would go on for an hour. Despite his pain, he stayed still.

After the spanking was done, I put the boy in the corner for ten minutes to reflect, pants and underpants still down for embarrassment. Afterward he apologized for his behavior. After that spanking I had no trouble from him for some time.

That was the first of many spankings I administered. I didn't look for opportunities to administer corporal punishment, but I was happy when they came along. I enjoyed punishing both boys and girls, although it was usually boys. They misbehaved much more than the girls.

With the younger children, the spankings were over the knee, bare bottom, and I spanked with my hand. I tried to reach a deep pink color, by which point they were crying and repentant.

With the older children, I also spanked over the knee, bare

bottom, but harder and longer, as I did with that first boy.

On a few occasions, I tried using a yardstick or switch on older children, with them bent over a desk. Judging from the dramatic responses of the children, who struggled to stay in place, these were *extremely* painful. With the yardstick, there were many parallel broad red raised lines across the bottom, which would be hot to the touch. With the switch — a great favorite in the hills and hollers — there'd be many bright red raised weals. Either one created a pretty picture on the unhappy recipient's bottom.

Still, I preferred simple over–the–knee hand spankings. I thought the position allowed me better to judge the "damage" I was doing as I could feel the bottom grow warmer and warmer with my hand. In addition, the children found the childish position more embarrassing, and that added to the punishment.

I found that my students preferred to be spanked rather than punished in other ways. In particular, keeping them after class was disruptive; it was a poor area and the youngsters had after–school jobs and chores to do at home, to help their families get by.

The punishments were always well–deserved; I always let close calls go. I never punished a student in front of others. In fact, I tried never to make a student lose face in any way in class. I never commented on the misbehavior or the spanking afterward; once the punishment was done; it was *done*. The students knew I cared for them and wanted to help them learn. No student ever refused when I told them they had to be spanked.

The parents backed me up completely and so did the School Board. I spent five wonderful years in that holler until I got a job offer from a famous prep school that was so good I had to accept it and double my salary. Unfortunately, corporal punishment was not permitted there, although some of the rich brats would have benefitted greatly from it.

X X X

AUNT'S HAIRBRUSH "GETS HER EXCITED"

— EMILY W., LONDON, ENGLAND

I am an English girl from the Midlands, in my first year as a nursing student in London. To save money I am living with an aunt at her flat near the hospital.

Recently she saw I was reading a book which she thought improper. She told me she would write to the head of the nursing school and my parents and tell them I was wasting my time and their tuition money reading pornography instead of working hard at my studies. (Which wasn't true; I was working hard and getting excellent marks.)

I said she was wrong, but knowing she could cause big problems, I said, "If I have to be punished, surely it can be some other way." She thought a moment, then told me she could, but it would mean "a discussion in the study." Since she was my father's sister, and my father used the same language, I knew what that meant. I went there as ordered, since I saw no way to escape the unfair punishment.

My aunt required me to remove my dress. To my embarrassment, she then made me lower my knickers. I was ordered to lie over her lap, and she spanked me severely with her hand and it smarted. I was happy when she stopped, but that was only so she could take up a hairbrush and return to her task. I cried, told her I couldn't stand the pain, and begged her to stop.

She said, "You should have thought of that when you took up

reading smut," and kept spanking.

When the spanking was over and I was putting my clothes on again my aunt continued to scold me and said she was going to throw out the book. However, a week later I noticed that she had not thrown it out, but was reading it herself. I jokingly said that since she was only ten years my elder, she deserved a spanking herself. She looked thoughtful, and after supper she told me to fetch her hairbrush.

I eagerly went, thinking that roles would be reversed and looking forward to spanking my very pretty aunt. But when I came back my aunt ordered me to stand in the corner facing the wall. That puzzled me. I thought perhaps she didn't want me to see her undressing for her spanking.

But then my aunt started lecturing me. Next I felt her raising my dress and pinning it above my waist. When I asked her what was going on, she said I had been impertinent and had earned another correction. I said "No." She said I should go to my bedroom and think it over carefully.

I only thought for a minute. I didn't want to provoke my aunt further and risk her sending letters to my school or parents or being thrown out of her flat, so I told her I was ready for my spanking.

Once more I had to pull everything down and get over my aunt's lap. I asked if I couldn't at least keep my panties on. I told her she could still spank me as hard as she wanted and as many times as she wished. But she said, "You will feel your correction better without them." So again I did as told, having no choice.

As with the first time, the spanking was painful right from the start. After a dozen smacks from my aunt's hand I was starting to cry despite my age. But at the same time something funny happened, as I felt myself getting excited in front despite the pain in back. It felt so good I didn't want her to stop. My bottom was in pain, but my front was all excited and shuddery. The more spanks my aunt gave, the better it felt. When she paused I hoped she hadn't finished and was happy when I felt her shift as she reached for the hairbrush. It felt even better as she finished my "correction" with what she liked to call her "correction tool."

Since that second spanking, late at night I have replayed it again and again. I have thought about how to earn more spankings without raising my aunt's suspicions and without risking her carrying out her threat to notify my school and parents about bad behavior. I want to be over her lap again, getting spanked and hairbrushed to cause the same wonderful feelings I had before.

I have decided to provoke a spanking by "relapsing" in my behavior and have purchased another steamy book for my aunt to accidentally discover.

I think if a girl is not being beaten, but just soundly spanked by someone who loves her and who she looks up to, it is certainly not abuse and can be very enjoyable and does "things" to her, causing the most amazing feelings. I think this is so even if the punishment is unfair, as it was in my case.

x x x

"TRADITIONAL PUNISHMENT" STILL DOES THE JOB FOR SPOUSES AND ADOLESCENTS

— MATT A., CHELTENHAM, U.K.

Regarding the letters, especially from young women, about being punished at home and in school, you might be interested in my experience. Years ago I worked for a company which supplied schools all over U.K. (and a select few foreign customers) with punishment canes, straps, tawses and birch rods (the birch rods locally only; customers wanted them fresh and they did not travel well).

At that time corporal punishment was common in schools. The teacher acting in the parent's place enjoyed the parent's authority over the person of the student. *In loco parentis*, as the Common Law used to put it, the teacher or principal would administer "reasonable" corporal chastisement with a suitable implement. Which my employer, owning about 16% market share, was happy to supply.

Of course today things are quite different. Although C.P. has almost disappeared from the schools, many parents are eager to enroll their children in the few private schools where the plimsoll, cane, tawse, or birch are still known.

I no longer work full time for that company, but still do some work for them in marketing, especially writing magazine adverts and advertising letters. This keeps me acquainted with their sources of customers.

Some of their business now comes from people who enjoy punishing each other, often in connection with sexual activity. Many of these are "confirmed bachelors" and "confirmed bachelorettes."

Most of their business, however, comes from parents. I see some of the letters from their customers, which usually start with "My [girl; boy] of [13, 14, 15 etc.] has become incorrigible of late." Then the parents describe the vandalism, gang behavior, acting out in school, staying out all night, associating with bad elements, or whatever. The letters usually end with an order for a particular punishment instrument.

Often, though, the writers seek advice: "Do you think a cane or tawse is more suitable for a misbehaving 15-year-old young miss? My husband and I have never punished our children this way. If it matters, our daughter has medium size buttocks."

These days the firm ships many orders to the United States. About 70% of sales to the States are Scottish tawses (split-tailed leather straps with handles). About 25% are canes. They've never caught on across the pond, have they? The remaining 5% are a miscellany: riding crops, carpet beaters, table tennis bats, large hairbrushes, hard plastic Lexan paddles, and whatever. As you can see, the firm has branched out far beyond what they used to supply to schools.

I'm sure some of your readers are customers of my firm. Perhaps they can describe their results using our canes and tawses. Personally I believe that the traditional "Six of the Best" or in extreme cases "Twelve of the Best" are an exceptionally persuasive form of correction for the average misbehaving teenager. And that the Scottish tawse is a close second in effectiveness.

By the way, tawses aren't always made by Scots; we have suppliers in Australia and the U.S.A. as well. But it is a special feeling to wield a tawse with a brand declaring, "Established in 1815."

It seems to me that past abuses of corporal punishment, especially where they sometimes led to scandalous behavior, caused not only a reaction, but an over-reaction to where it has virtually disappeared from schools. But the experience of our firm shows that there are many parents, even in this "modern" generation, who trust in traditional means of correction. I hope to see more letters about their experiences, the methods they used, and the results. I'd especially like to hear from the adolescent objects of their corrections.

CANINGS, BIRCHINGS, STRAPPINGS AT HER GIRLS' REFORMATORY

— MARGARET N., DURHAM, NORTH CAROLINA

I was born and raised in Merrie Olde England by strict, no–nonsense parents. I attended British girls' schools that were very strictly run. British Common Law did not allow a teacher to administer corporal punishment *unless* the parent's consent was obtained. However, it was a *condition* of admission to the schools I attended that parents give consent to "reasonable and customary corporal punishment short of causing injury."

Today, as I understand matters, corporal punishment is barred in all government schools. And for other schools, British legislation as well as Common Law bars school corporal punishment *except* with parental consent. However, many parents will gladly give such consent.

It is true that such classical instruments of corporal punishment as the cane and birch are sold in many British shops, and of course many more are probably sold through the privacy of the internet. However, I believe that more corporal punishment (of any sort) is imposed on younger children than their adolescent elders, and more on boys than girls.

Furthermore, few parents, I think, use a cane or birch on a girl older than twelve. More parents in England (and some parts of Europe) use corporal punishment than here in the States, but these days a slipper, tawse or yardstick is more commonly applied to the girl's bottom than a cane or birch. Also, some parents use the Yankee paddle, so popular in American schools; that was almost unknown in England years ago and is still rare.

Unless a girl has legally become a ward of the state, such as being remanded to a school of correction (typically between ages 13 and 18), she cannot be physically chastised by a superior without her parents' approval. Even then, there are invariably strict rules and procedures for such punishment. If the punishment is applied with a flexible instrument, such as the tawse [split—tailed leather spanking strap, originating in Scotland — Ed.] she must be standing with her right side against a wall, lying flat on a table, or in some other posture that keeps the strap from curling around her buttocks and striking where it shouldn't.

I am familiar with this whole subject because I taught sewing at an institution for wayward girls. Copies of the institution's rules and disciplinary policy were given to all employees, as well as to the girls and the parents of girls committed to such places. In addition, I observed a number of punishments. I never actually punished the girl but was there as an observer or "chaperone." Let me describe the procedures still in force where I worked. I believe it to be typical of such institutions throughout England.

A nurse, male or female, is present. No other men should be present except the person doing the punishing, and even there women are preferred where possible. The highest person in authority at the institution should be present, or if unavailable her immediate inferior. The presence of a female "chaperone" or observer (my role now and then) is encouraged though not required. The offender may not be undressed more than is necessary, which means only her buttocks and upper thighs are nude.

The girl may be punished only on the buttocks, the buttocks—thighs crease, and, in the case of the birch, the upper thighs as well. No more than 18 strokes of the tawse or birch, or 12 of the cane or paddle, can be administered within one week. (Those numbers were in force at the institutions where I taught; the rules may vary slightly elsewhere.) A girl may not be punished if she still displays "damage" from a previous correction.

These numbers were the absolute maximums; most punishments were half those, and corporal punishment was rare. It was reserved for serious breaches, and even then usually only after a series of faults when lesser punishments proved ineffective.

I remember the daughter of a friend being committed to my establishment for six months as a guest of the Crown for repeated truancy and other mischief. Her parents were surprised by the rules and their girl was terrified. They asked me many questions about life inside those walls. In fact the girl stayed out of trouble there and was never even disciplined in any way, let alone punished on her body.

I have seen descriptions of canings by some of your other correspondents, and they sound implausible. They do not match what I observed.

For one thing, the descriptions make it sound like a caning is not much worse than an ordinary spanking that a single parent might administer. Not so. Even one of the smaller teen age girls at my place would require at least one matron to hold her in place while she was getting the cane; if her sentence was "a dozen of the best," she would often require two matrons. A caning feels as if a long burning wire is being placed on the skin and held there. It is agonizing when the stroke lands and the pain lasts and lasts. Even if the girl does her best to stay in position, her body reacts to each stroke, twisting and bucking.

During my stay there the head got so tired of canings requiring extra staff help that they took to strapping the girls down for punishment. They used a sort of saddle that the girl would bend over, raising and tightening her buttocks. Her hands, ankles and waist would be secured with straps. Once the girl was in position, there was no escape, and extra help was not needed. I understand that this revived the way things were done in Victorian and Edwardian times.

Another writer says that the results (of a caning) "quickly fade away without injury or mark." I agree that there is no permanent injury, but it takes some time for the results to "fade away!"

As far as marks, when a girl received six strokes, a skillful punisher could lay them all parallel, without any crossing over.

That is the ideal, and some experienced practitioners could do it every time, even when a girl had small buttocks. However, with twelve strokes, it is almost impossible to apply them even to a large girl's buttocks without some strokes striking the same spot twice. When that happens — the cane landing on already–welted skin, the girl usually gets small red marks that take a *long* time to fade. Even longer where an entire stroke lands perfectly on top of a previous stroke line. This causes another level of pain, judging from the girls' emphatic reactions; it invariably reduces even the bravest girl to uncontrolled crying.

One of the reasons girls *must* be bared for their punishment is so that the person wielding the cane (or birch) can see what he's doing and try to avoid striking the same spot on the buttocks twice. The nudity is not just for humiliation, although that certainly is an important element of the dreaded punishment.

A birch has a similar effect to the cane. Though the birch strikes over a much larger area than the cane, the punisher still tries to keep the strokes as far apart as possible and avoid striking the same flesh twice. As with the cane, it may be possible or almost possible if the girl is only getting six; but it's impossible with twelve.

Unlike with the cane, birching was done on both the buttocks and upper thighs. In any case, with either the birch or the cane, the descriptions from other writers of single parent punishment are difficult to credit. It is hard to expect that a girl will — or is able to! — stay still without straps or additional persons keeping her there.

Finally, as to the people comparing the favored instruments in England with those in the States, I believe many instruments are satisfactory. Most of the American parents I know are capable of enforcing discipline with the traditional hairbrush, belt, paddle or switch, without having to import canes or tawses, let alone figure out how to maintain a supply of birches, which must be fresh to be safe and useful.

x x x

"THE HOTTER MY BACKSIDE, THE HOTTER FOR SEX"

— ERICA H., DRUMMONDVILLE, QUEBEC, CANADA

I am a self–sufficient, well–educated 25–year–old woman who makes more than my fiancé. As he is very careless with money his wages go straight into my account and I deal with the bills for both of us. We're both happy with this, as we are saving a lot of money and manage with the remaining disposable income.

In short, I am very careful, conservative, sensible and "controlling" as far as money is concerned. My fiancé happily submits to my authority and expertise.

In the bedroom, however, roles are reversed. He is a tiger, and I am submissive in a dominance/submission (D&S), bondage discipline sadomasochism (BDSM), top/bottom sort of way. This, too, makes both of us happy. I am never more ready for sex than after I've been firmly put over my fiancé's knee, bared of any cover for my nether areas, and spanked with his hand until I can't cry any more. The hotter my backside, the hotter I am for sex. Spanking me has the same effect on my fiancé: nothing gets him more excited.

We have tried over the lap spanking with hairbrushes, sawed–off bath brushes, several flat paint stirrer sticks glued together, and other things.

We have also tried having me bend over furniture, while my fiancé uses a wooden paddle, leather shaving strop and other things on me. But we always come back to over the lap with his hand, which is more than enough for a good "warming."

If people wanted to watch, I'd be fine with that, although my fiancé isn't. If we could find people to pay to watch me be spanked, that would be great with me! We'd save money a lot faster.

I know many girls who enjoy being spanked by their husbands or boyfriends.

x x x

BIG SURPRISE AT GROUP BIRTHDAY SPANKING

— WENDY M., SLEEPY EYE, MINNESOTA

I am surprised the letters make so little mention of that glorious, uniquely American tradition — the birthday spanking or paddling. Although my family did not practice that custom when I grew up, I was introduced to it recently.

My husband and I arranged to rent a lakeside cottage for two weeks this summer. As it happens, my birthday fell in the middle of that fortnight. But my husband and I hadn't planned anything special except a romantic late night dinner — or so I thought.

On my birthday I took a long swim in the lake. Afterwards I went back to the cottage, took off my bathing suit, and rinsed the sand off the suit and me under a screened outdoor shower at the back of the cottage. Then, as I usually did, I hung the suit and my towel to dry near the shower, and went into the cottage wearing nothing but earrings.

As soon as I closed the door there was a loud chorus of cheers and "Happy Birthday, Joan!" My husband and four couples who are our close friends had organized a surprise birthday party!

Well, I was certainly surprised, and so was everyone else, especially the men. For a moment everyone was pop-eyed and silent; then they all started laughing. They considered my embarrassment a big joke. All I could do was laugh along with them. In

38

fact I joined in the spirit by striking a few burlesque poses before heading toward my bedroom to get something on.

I was almost there when someone said I hadn't had my birthday spanking yet even though I had been helpful enough to get ready and strip. I tried to escape to the bedroom but was outnumbered. My husband should have stopped the nonsense but he was too busy laughing. So I didn't have a chance.

With my husband's approval, each of the men, cheered on by the women, put me over his lap and gave me my age, 20 spanks. It was terribly painful after a while, though the last ones took it easier, seeing I was already red, sore and crying. My husband was about to put me over his lap, too, but had mercy on me. The others teased and goaded him on, but he said they'd all done a good job, so he would save his birthday spanking for a few days later, after I had recovered.

Only after my bottom was bright cherry red, burning in pain and hot to the touch (all the women felt it and marveled), was I allowed to escape and get some clothes on and put my face together after all the crying. I wore my loosest, thinnest shorts, without panties; my bottom hurt so much I could hardly stand the touch of fabric. When I came out, everyone congratulated me on taking my birthday spanking so well. Then we had barbecue and birthday cake and I got presents.

During the spanking I could think only of the pain and indignity, and get furious at my husband for not protecting me. After the spanking, although I enjoyed the party, I was still suffering from both the pain and the humiliation. But looking back and reliving the spankings, a few days afterward as well as now, I feel differently. I can still feel those spankings, one after another, like waves of pain, and my humiliated feelings at being exposed by all those men in front of a crowd. However, there was also something incredibly exciting about having to lie helplessly and obediently over their laps and having them spank me so painfully. I know that in that position everyone could see everything I had.

My husband and the whole bunch tease me about my spanking whenever we get together. They say it was so much fun they intend to repeat it next year with a paddle they've bought for the purpose. The women say the men hogged the fun and it's *their* turn to spank me next year.

My husband just says "Hmm." I know he'd say "no" to their plans if I insist, but I'm thinking it might be fun, so maybe I should let it happen. I wonder whether it would be more exciting to be spanked by the women than the men. Maybe one of your readers can advise.

One other thing. My husband kept his promise to give me *his* special birthday spanking after I recovered. Each day after my birthday he made me drop my panties so he could inspect my bottom, both looking at and feeling every inch. Five days later he pronounced it good as new and I was soon over his lap, getting another twenty with his hand on *each* bottom side, which I thought wasn't really part of the bargain. Then I got another bunch of spanks, each on both sides, for luck, health, wealth, happiness and so on and on. Getting blistered by my dear husband was just as painful, but even more exciting, than getting it from our friends, and we had wild sex right afterward.

x x x

MEMORABLE CORPORAL PUNISHMENTS ARE EROTICALLY EXCITING

— M. A., SAN DIEGO, CALIFORNIA

The many letters and articles you have published about true spanking, paddling and other physical punishment experiences have given me the courage to tell about my own experiences. For years I've wished to share my background, but didn't do so with close friends for fear they would make fun of me. But I am willing to do so in print if my name isn't used.

My parents died when I was only 6 years old, and I was raised by my sister, who was 12 years older than me — 18 at the time I was orphaned. I was upset by my parents' death, sought attention a lot, including negative attention, and ended up being a mischievous troublemaker. My sister, though loving, was also strict, as my parents had been, and used spankings and whippings as her "first and last resort" for misbehavior and disobedience.

When I was younger, she would take down my pants and underpants, put me over her lap and spank me with her hand until my poor buttocks were bright red and I was crying and promising to behave. Then I'd be sent to stand against the wall for 5 minutes.

As I got older, I got switched. After taking down everything, my sister would make me bend over a sofa arm, resting my head on my arms. She would then whip me with a switch made of several twigs from bushes in our back yard. I was the one who had to go back and choose the twigs for my own punishment, a humiliating ordeal because sometimes the neighbors or their children would see me and make jokes.

Those switchings were agony; anyone who has ever been switched knows a long, well–cut switch doesn't just hurt; it burns like fire and keeps burning for hours, especially the lower part of the buttocks and thighs. I would always try not to cry, but never succeeded. I blubbered like a baby and begged my sister to stop long before she decided I'd had enough.

After the switching and the corner time, my sister would let me suffer for several hours. Then, *if* she felt I had "taken my whipping well," she would come to my room, tell me to lie down on my stomach, pull everything down again, and hold an ice pack on my striped buttocks. Sometimes she would put a lotion on them that dulled the pain. Meanwhile she'd quietly talk to me about my misbehavior.

When I got older and was strong enough to resist, she would tie my hands first, then force me over furniture for my switching. If I'd given her a hard time, she'd switch me even worse, and there was no ice or lotion for relief afterward.

These switchings, which she called "whippings" by the way, went on until I was 14, when my sister's husband told her I was getting too big to be bared in front of my sister, especially since I had gotten an erection during a whipping. He also didn't approve of the lotion massage afterward. I had also gotten well–behaved by that time. Anyhow, the switchings finally stopped.

After I graduated from high school by the skin of my teeth, I joined the Navy to "see the world," as the old recruiting slogan said. I was not a model recruit, and several times during boot camp I ended up under lock and key and unfortunately renewed my acquaintance with whipping. Those punishments made my sister's switchings seem like child's play. I may have gone into detention like a lion, but I came out like a lamb.

First, I was ordered to strip naked. Then I was bent over a desk and my hands tied to the other side so I was tightly held. Then an M.P. stuck his finger in my rectum and wiggled it around, and that hurt. He said he was making sure I hadn't smuggled a machine gun into the lockup. Then I got punished.

One time I tried to get out of the punishment by claiming I was feeling sick. The M.P.'s brought in a medic who checked my blood pressure and heart rate, stuck a thermometer in my rectum and said I was good to go. If anything, the M.P.'s punished me worse that time for faking and wasting their time.

As far as the punishment itself, with me bent over and completely exposed, I was whipped with a leather strap until I cried and begged them to stop. My buttocks ended up horribly red and swollen. After the strapping was finished, they would hose me down with cold water, and then return me to my cell and throw my clothes in after me.

As painful and humiliating as these punishments were, punishments which I would never want to repeat, I found they caused very strange and disturbing feelings afterward, mixed in with the pain. I didn't want to recognize these as what they were — erotic excitement caused by the strapping. I was worried that would mean I was a pervert or a "queer." Gays were called "queers" or "fruits" or worse at that place, and would find themselves getting beaten up.

I ended up not seeing the world. I served at the naval base in San Diego my whole hitch, and the closest I got to seeing the world was visiting the Mexican border town of Tijuana many times.

Parts of San Diego were such that our officers warned us only to visit them in groups rather than alone; ask anyone what Horton Plaza was like before they knocked everything down and turned it into a sterile mall. But Tijuana was *wide open*; you could get anything there. If you wanted a 14–year–old girl, you could have one. All those jokes about "my leetle seester" were based on reality. If you wanted a boy rather than a girl, you could have that too.

There were shows in Tijuana where you could watch a woman doing it with a donkey, something I had always assumed was impossible until I saw it with my own eyes. There were also shows where you could watch a woman being whipped; you'd find those if you asked around, especially if you knew a little Spanish. I went to those and they got me excited. Tijuana has been cleaned up, too; Old Tijuana, like Old San Diego, are golden memories.

After I left the Navy, I fell head over heels for a rich, spoiled, beautiful, strong willed girl. Until then I had been very successful with women, and was the boss with my girlfriends. But this girl had me under her thumb.

Soon after I met this girl, I read a book about men who liked to be whipped and dominated by women. I was shocked and amazed. The book awakened memories of my feelings all those times my sister had whipped me with a switch. Where the book included the men's descriptions of their feelings during a whipping and afterward, I thought, "That's me!"

"Were there really millions of men who felt this way?" I wondered.

I showed the book to my girlfriend. Unlike me, she wasn't shocked or amazed. She said I must have lived a sheltered life if I hadn't heard about such things before. She said such feelings were common, and in fact she had known boyfriends who liked to be spanked, whipped and paddled.

That conversation didn't go any farther. Soon after, though, I got my girlfriend upset. She'd already been upset because I'd started getting messy in her apartment — things like reading the newspaper and leaving it on the couch instead of throwing it out, and shaving without cleaning up the bathroom sink behind me. The last straw came when I showed up late to take her out, *and* I'd already had a drink or two. (I'd already had one DUI beef that I was lucky to beat.)

Anyhow, my girlfriend was furious and threatened to break up. "You deserve to be whipped," she said.

I didn't want to lose her, and I knew I was at fault anyhow, and her words turned on a switch in my head.

"Maybe you're right," I said. "Do you think that would clear things up?"

She looked at me thoughtfully and oddly, thought for a moment, then said, "On second thought, come inside."

I didn't know what to expect. More outbursts? The silent

treatment? Was I still in for a breakup? I started to apologize some more, but she said, "Just stay there," and left.

In a minute my girlfriend returned, and this time she was carrying a long horse riding crop. She said she thought a little whipping was what I needed to change my behavior and treat her with respect, and since I had agreed, that was what I was going to get. I couldn't say anything, but stared at the crop in fear, shock, nervousness — and behind those, weird feelings of excitement.

I told my girlfriend I was not going to let myself get whipped, but it must have been obvious I was in two minds. I probably didn't sound very convincing. I wasn't sure how I felt; despite my fear I was getting more and more excited. She told me it was either submit myself to a whipping "to clear things up," or look for another girlfriend. So I gave in and said I'd allow her to punish me.

She told me she was going to whip me, not my pants, so get everything off. Feeling more and more nervous, I took off my shirt, then my pants and stood there in my undershorts. She told me I was not going to get any protection and ordered me to take those off too. Reluctantly I did as told.

Then she said that since I might change my mind or not be able to stay still, for my safety she was going to secure me by tying my hands and feet. After doing so with my own neckties, she bent me over a footstool. There was no way I was going anywhere. I was very excited, and I was already getting an erection. I was getting the same feelings I had when my sister had tied my hands to make me helpless before switching me. Bent over like that, nude, penis, balls, hole and buttocks completely exposed, I was very excited by my submission. She left me for a moment to get a towel, and put that under my penis. She said, "I'm not going to have you make a mess."

Then my girlfriend proceeded to whip me severely with her riding crop, and she was not only strong, but a real expert. She lashed me mostly on my buttocks, but a little bit on the upper thighs and especially on that sensitive crease where thighs turn into buttocks. I heard each lash coming, since it made a humming sound in the air. An instant later I would feel the burning line across my buttock cheeks.

The punishment was not brutal, but it was hard enough and long enough and painful enough to remind me that I was not the boss in our relationship and she expected to be treated with respect. As she whipped me she said if I misbehaved again we would have more sessions like this until I learned my lesson. By the time she finished, my poor buttocks were crisscrossed with angry red raised welts that burned for a long time. And unlike my sister, she didn't believe in putting anything on them to soothe the pain, either.

That evening changed our relationship. I realized my desire, that I had tried to pretend to myself didn't exist, had been satisfied by the whipping. In fact, I'd had a tremendous orgasm all over the towel during the whipping. I was eager to repeat the session, and gave my girlfriend excuses to punish me at every opportunity. Every time was both humiliating and incredibly exciting sexually. Even though I would usually come during the punishment, we almost always had sex afterwards as well. Whipping me turned her on almost as much as me.

We have now been married several years and we are quite happy in our sex life. No one knows that my wife punishes me this way, or that we use it to get us both excited for sex.

We have a house now. It has a basement apartment, but we don't rent that out; the whole apartment is set up for punishment. We have a whipping saddle, consisting of an old riding saddle attached to a low sawhorse. I am put over that sideways, hands and feet attached to the sawhorse legs. I am always naked. That position also leaves me completely exposed so that my wife can do anything else she wants to me.

We also have another treasure, a modern doctor's examining table, complete with stirrups. The table can be cranked into all kinds of open, humiliating positions suitable for whipping and other punishment, and the medical setting is exciting.

My wife uses all kinds of things on me. In addition to the riding crop, she has a buggy whip, a razor strap, a school principal's type of paddle, and a "cat–o'–nine–tails" with nine thin rubber strips attached to a handle. We don't have any tree or bush suitable for switches, but now and then when we go hiking we'll cut switches for later use on me.

Sometimes my wife will put me over her knee and paddle me with a hairbrush. I like that intimate position. But usually I'm over the spanking saddle downstairs in that humiliating head down, buttocks up and open position.

Interestingly, in every other aspect of our marriage, we are equals or indeed I am the boss; my wife does not try to exert her authority. Only in the basement am I reduced to the posture of a little boy, being humiliated and soundly punished.

We are very happy with each other and feel what we do in our home is our own business and no one has the right to judge whether we are "normal" or "different." Our relationship, above stairs and below stairs, suits us perfectly and we have a wonderful sex life.

x x x

SPANKED BY FRIEND'S WIFE

— HAROLD N., BOSTON, MASSACHUSETTS

Congratulations on helping bring this exciting sexual activity [spanking] out of the closet. Your book is both courageous and enlightening.

I have also been intrigued by recent surveys showing a widespread interest in spanking. I think some of these even underestimate the interest by forcing those surveyed to disclose their names. Even though the surveyor promises to keep their identity confidential, most people are still hesitant to tell the whole story about their practices.

One aspect in which surveys seem to differ quite a bit is the percentage of men versus women who spank or are spanked. It would be interesting to know what percentage of the letters you get on the subject have dealt with spanking of men and what percentage have dealt with spanking of women, and whether each sex is mostly spanking or being spanked.

I am interested in this question, of course, because of my own experiences. I spanked several girlfriends playfully before I got married. I have also spanked my wife several times with my hand. Normally playfully, but the ones she gets each year on her birthday have been "for real." However, it is usually I who takes the punishment and my wife who deals it out.

We became interested in spanking when we met another rather freewheeling young couple around our own age. We all became good friends. The man admitted to us that his wife treats him as a virtual slave, including spanking him hard, as foreplay to sex, and that they both enjoy it hugely.

Inspired by our friends, my wife and I began to try out spanking, and I soon developed an appetite for being spanked. We told our friends about our experiments and they were delighted. In fact, they suggested we all try it out together, and we've done so about a dozen times.

When we get together his wife spanks me and my wife spanks him. One of us is spanked at a time. The others watch as he is stripped, spoken to as a slave, forced to do various submissive acts, and finally tied down to a piece of furniture and soundly spanked. To emphasize the slave role, we men are sometimes made to wear simple tunics, as Greek slave boys might have worn. I emphasize, however, that there is no sex involved. We are not "wife–swappers." We do not have an "open marriage."

The manner of spanking — how hard, instruments used, the spanked man's posture — is completely up to the spanker, short of causing physical harm, of course. My wife likes to punish our friend with a 3–tailed leather strap called a tawse, specially made for punishment. We bought it from a company in Dundee, Scotland. It's amazing to see my friend's buttocks turn pink, then red, then deep red under the tawse. He is always reduced to a state of sobbing. He can't really move his buttocks out of the way, but he has enough room to tremble and shake.

At the same time, he becomes visibly excited by the whipping. When he is let up he sometimes has a total erection, and if so he and his wife repair to a bedroom for "relief."

When I am spanked, my friend's wife has also used the tawse, as well as a cane, school paddle and a yardstick. Tied down nude in a bent over posture, I am acutely aware that three people can see everything I have. My friend's wife likes to take her time with the spanking, spending long pauses to tease and lecture her "slave boy." The spanking is very, very painful, but exciting at the same time. I think the excitement is half psychological, half physical. By the end my buttocks are burning, and I am sobbing under this strong woman's ministrations as much as my friend does at the hands of my wife.

One time my friend's wife complained that I was squirming around too much and needed to stay still. I don't think that was really true; she just wanted an excuse to embarrass me in a different way. To encourage me to stay still, she produced a "butt plug," a six inch long solid rubber device shaped like a penis but less thick.

Our rule is no sexual touching, so she couldn't insert it in me. Instead she handed it to my wife. My wife was reluctant at first, but with the other woman coaching her, she lubricated the plug, slowly worked it into me, and taped it in place. With the plug solidly fixed, along with being whipped, I had an erection that wouldn't quit. Every time the strap landed, the plug would jiggle around in me and rub on my prostate. Psychologically, it is amazing how a few ounces of rubber can make me feel total slave–like submission.

After that whipping, my friend's wife left me in position, plug still in place, while the three of them sat around having fruit and coffee and joking about the condition of my behind.

My wife and I are both 26 and have been married two years. The other couple is our age but have been married since he was 18 and she was 17. They are experienced in many sexual activities and "sidelines" and constantly try new ones.

x x x

THE SPANKING PHOTO THAT CHANGED THEIR LIVES

— HAROLD N., BOSTON, MASSACHUSETTS

My wife and I met at work a year after graduating from different colleges nearby. We were alike in many ways. Both of us live in the "world of the mind," she as a manuscript editor, me as a graphic designer for textbooks. Both of us had led sheltered lives, even at college; neither of us had ever used drugs except for the occasional bit of pot to try to fit in with our peers and neither of us had ever been drunk. Both of us were inexperienced sexually compared to our contemporaries and had never explored anything but vanilla intercourse. You could say we had overdeveloped our intellectual natures — in addition to our work, our main hobbies were crossword puzzles and Bridge — but neglected our emotional, physical and sexual sides.

On our first dates, this situation didn't change, and although we felt more and more we were suited to each other, there was no excitement. One night I brought her home from a date to her house, which she shared with three other women, and unlike the previous times, she asked me in for a drink.

I had to go to the bathroom, and was surprised to find a framed photo on the counter. The frame was titled "Girl of the Week." The photo showed my girlfriend lying across the lap of one of her housemates, wearing only a slip which was pulled above her waist and panties which were pulled below her but-tocks. The other girl's hand held a hairbrush poised just above my girlfriend's buttocks, and those buttocks were bright, glow-ing, cherry red. In addition, I could glimpse my girl's beaver and her orifice in back. That's was a lot more than I'd seen so far; all we'd done was some kissing and petting over clothing.

Surprised and embarrassed, I left the bathroom quickly, leav-ing the photo on the counter. As I was coming out of the bath-room, one of the girls was going in and yelled, "Omigod!" Then she started laughing and said, "The cat's out of the bag."

My girlfriend and her housemate then sat down with me and told me the housemates enforced good behavior with corporal punishment. They kept a "Demerit Log" in the form of a large of-ficial looking hard covered ledger. Different faults earned differ-ent numbers of demerits for the girl who erred. Demerits were earned for things like not cleaning up after themselves, forget-ting assigned chores, disturbing others late at night, or leaving without setting the burglar alarm.

Every Wednesday the girl with the most demerits earned a hairbrush paddling and had her picture posted until the next Wednesday as a reminder and to encourage good behavior by all of them. They were supposed to put away the photo for com-pany, but they forgot.

The girls behaved about equally well or badly, so on average each got spanked about once a month. The number of smacks depended on the number of demerits, but was usually about 30, 15 on each butt cheek. That would keep the girl sore for a day and red for two days. They had chosen Wednesdays as punish-ment night so the girl would look normal for Friday and week-end dates.

The idea of my girlfriend and her pretty housemates spanking each other fascinated me. I found myself thinking about my girl in all kinds of new ways. I wanted to see and experience for real what the picture had only shown.

I was given the gift of an excuse a few weeks later, when my girlfriend totally forgot our dinner date. She had to work late — I didn't blame her for that — but forgot to call me. When we made another date, I told her, "Afterwards we'll discuss this matter at my place," leaving her to think about that.

After that dinner, back at my apartment, I told my girl that she had earned a good spanking for such inconsiderate behavior. Even though she knew she was in the wrong, she struggled, but soon enough I had her firmly over my knee. She delayed but couldn't prevent me from getting her skirt rucked up and her panties down to her knees. She kept struggling but none of it helped free her. I told her if she kept it up, she'd just get worse. Yielding to the inevitable, she and lay obediently in the classic position of a child about to be spanked.

I then gave her about twenty hard smacks with my hand. I'd never spanked a girl before, and some of them didn't land squarely, or landed on the thighs more than the buttocks. I just laughed to myself, "That one didn't count" and aimed better next time. Soon I had her yelping and pleading for mercy.

She wasn't crying enough, so I reached for a hairbrush, which I had bought specially that day and hidden next to the couch. Those dozen hard smacks with the brush got a much louder response than the twenty with my hand. Finally my girl broke down into continuous, uncontrolled crying. Even after stopping the hairbrush spanking, I kept her over my lap for five minutes. I reveled in her bright red, blotched cheeks. I kept feeling them; they were incredibly hot to the touch. She lay obediently over my lap. I could tell she was seething from the spanking, the submissive posture, and the liberties I was taking.

When I let her up, she was furious. But she instantly calmed down when I held her and said she was welcome to a return trip over my knee if she kept up her fussing. A little later that evening she said she'd started to take our relationship for granted, and admitted she deserved the spanking for standing me up and maybe it did her some good.

That evening put our relationship on a different level. After the spanking we were much closer. We went together for another six months, doing the usual things people do. The only unusual thing was that I spanked my girlfriend about once a week. That's probably unusual for people engaged to be married.

Spankings are still common in our relationship. Usually they are for small faults, but if my wife's behavior has been perfect, I'll contrive some excuse. I use my hand, but sometimes follow with the hairbrush. We still have the same hairbrush that cemented our relationship. The spankings are hard enough to get her buttocks reddened and hot; she cries and begs me to stop.

Now and then my wife actually gives me good reason to spank her. Those spankings are hard, long and with the hairbrush. Although she can't really move, held as she is over my knee, there's a lot of shaking and buttocks jiggling as each hairbrush smack lands. By the end she is bright, glowing, fiery hot red, the crying is for real, not for show, and the apologizing and begging is desperate.

Nine of ten spankings are with me spanking my wife. But occasionally, when I have done something very wrong, the tables have been turned. The first time my wife laid into me with the hairbrush, I chickened out. I resisted and got away as I am bigger and stronger than she is. After looking at a magazine about sexual spanking, we solved that problem. Although I have to consent to the spanking (which I do; I've earned every one), she is put in complete control and I have no way to change my mind in the middle.

Our means is two simple leather wrist cuffs, of the sort used for restraining insane people in asylums. These are put on me. Each has a metal ring, so my bound wrists can each be attached to a piece of furniture, or brought close and attached to it together. With my wrists controlled, I am as helplessly under her control as she would be under mine, and she takes full advantage of her superiority.

Sometimes I am bent upside down over a couch arm, while my wife stands behind me and punishes me. More usually she will cuff my hands together, behind me, then choose a more intimate position by putting me over her knee. As I feel my pants, then my underwear, descend below my knees, and on hot days the breeze from a floor fan on my buttocks, I feel humiliatingly exposed and realize the last shred of dignity and protection is gone. I get the same helpless feelings I did when I was a boy of twelve, in the same position over my mother's lap. My wife will squeeze and pat my buttocks, as well as caress other male parts nearby, before taking up the hairbrush.

After a brief lecture, she will punish me. Typically I get 40 to 50 blistering whacks, depending on what I did, and more if she decides I'm not taking my spanking properly. I am always reduced to sobbing and repentance soon after the punishment starts, but it keeps on for what seems like forever no matter how many tears I shed. I can almost feel my buttocks blistering.

The pain and color last for days. But clearing the air by me atoning and her dispelling her upset feelings, keeps our relationship perfect.

I think many times of how that photograph, and the coincidence of one of the girls forgetting to put it away, changed my life. It charged my erotic feelings for my girlfriend and led to me spanking her, which changed our relationship completely. If not for that picture, would we ever have discovered this possibility? Would we have never really ignited any erotic passion, even when married?

x x x

HUMILIATING THRASHINGS CHANGE HER BEHAVIOR

— CHARLOTTE N., SWINDON, U.K.

I was born in Leeds but grew up in London and graduated from a famous university there, though I also spent some time at a smaller London university and an American university in Boston.

When I was 17½ my parents had to go overseas and I was left in the care of a widowed aunt, my father's sister. She was a school administrator and sometime teacher. I attended the local university. To be frank, my aunt didn't really keep close tabs on me. For awhile I had a very active social life, including keeping irregular hours. I told my aunt I was studying late at the library. My marks, although good, were not what they could have been. I had also taken to skipping classes, using excuses such as illness, where they impinged on my social calendar.

As it turned out, one of my lecturers happened to know my aunt, and knew that I was staying with her. He ran into my aunt one morning and asked her whether I was feeling better, and the whole story came out about me missing classes. My aunt, who knew I hadn't been ill, was surprised and very upset. To make things worse, that night I came in very late. I gave my usual excuse, but my aunt had found out the library actually had closed two hours earlier.

My aunt had stayed up waiting for me and insisted on an explanation for my "disgraceful behavior." She said I was throwing away my parents' and her money (she was helping them with my tuition and expenses) and that she was planning to get reports from all my lecturers and then write my parents.

I begged my aunt not to tell my parents. I pleaded with her to be punished some other way. At first she was firm, but finally she decided on — spanking. She ordered me to go to her room and I had no choice but to obey.

My aunt ordered me to take off my skirt and girdle, and lie on the bed. Again I did as ordered. I assumed she would use her hand or a hairbrush or slipper, but she said I deserved a strap.

She opened the closet and pulled out a heavy leather strap with twin tails. The reddish–brown horror was more than two feet long, plus handle. She told me to take my panties down. I didn't want to, but she said if she had to help me, my punishment would be worse, so I raised up and skinned them down to my knees. That didn't satisfy her and she pulled them right off.

My aunt lectured me about ten minutes and then started my strapping. I had never been punished this way before; no more than a few hand slaps on my pantied bottom when I was young. The strap was terribly painful right from the start and I began howling. My aunt said I'd wake the neighbors and brought a towel for me to hold in my mouth. Then she resumed. She lectured me between strokes. I wasn't counting, but she told me afterward she'd given me 18 strokes. With all the lecturing, my strapping took more than half an hour. My whole bum was red as apples, swollen and throbbing with pain, and I bawled for a long time.

My aunt was kind toward me afterward, but very firm. I also learned that this punishment was only the *first* installment. And indeed, she strapped me again the same way a week later and again a week after that.

After that, things calmed down. I still went out at night sometimes, but only with my aunt's permission. I made sure never to miss class, and mostly stopped slacking on my schoolwork.

However, a few months later I veered off the tracks again. I'd been at a wild party and forgotten the time, stumbling in hours later than expected. Even in my state, I knew what was coming the moment I saw my aunt's face.

This time my aunt didn't even bother with the lecture. (I got it the next day.) She ordered me to fetch the strap. There is no feeling like being sent to fetch the means of your own punishment at 2:00 in the morning. This time my aunt made me take off every stitch and lie down over the couch arm. She told me this time my punishment would be worse because apparently my previous punishments hadn't done the job.

That punishment *was* worse. With me bend double over the couch arm, my bottom was tightened up, no slack at all, so I felt every stroke of the strap deeply. Also, my aunt was more experienced by now. Finally, she gave me *twenty–four* agonizingly painful strokes. I bawled into my towel the whole time and long afterward.

I got a reminder dose a week later, too. After that punishment, my aunt told me that next time I misbehaved, she'd thrash me even worse. Then she took me into the bathroom and showed me an large enema bag with a frightening large black nozzle. She told me next time she'd not only strap me, but give me a "punishment enema with strong soapsuds," wash my mouth out with soap, and make me write lines. I knew she meant every word. I managed to stay out of trouble the next few months until I moved out of her flat.

Those were the only times I got a thrashing. Every one of those thrashings was extremely painful, and acutely humiliating as well. My poor behind stayed crimson and burned for some time afterward. Unlike some other correspondents, I felt absolutely no pleasure in my humiliating punishments and certainly no erotic excitement. I did not enjoy those punishments, and did everything possible to avoid any more.

My aunt, satisfied with the improvement in my behavior, never told my parents about my misbehavior or my punishments.

x x x

SPANKING EACH OTHER TRANSFORMS THEIR MARRIAGE

— ELWOOD R., INDIANA

My wife and I live in a large city in Indiana. I have an excellent job with a well known company. We have a very happy marriage relationship. The letters [in your publications] have been very illuminating and reassure us that we are not the only couple which enjoys spankings.

Soon after we married, my wife and I discovered, to our surprise, that spanking got us very excited sexually and usually led to sexual intercourse right away. I say we were surprised because here's how we happened to discover this turn–on.

After our honeymoon we settled in to married life, and unfortunately started to have friction. The usual little disagreements got worse until we found ourselves going for days giving each other the silent treatment. Less than six months after our marriage, we were both frustrated by these constant disagreements, and at the point of looking for a marriage counselor.

Out of the blue, my wife said to me, "Why do we drive ourselves crazy this way? The answer is simple. When one of us has done something wrong, why don't we just agree that the other one inflicts some sort of punishment and clears the air in a hurry? We can agree on some form of punishment."

I agreed. After some talking it out, we decided to use the

punishment we both had suffered when we misbehaved as children. That is, old–fashioned spanking. I admit that there was some awkwardness and embarrassment the first few times each of us suffered this humiliating "correction," but we found that it did cut our quarrels short and led to a much better relationship. So we agreed that we had taken a wise step and continued the arrangement.

At first we agreed to try it for three months and review the results. When the three months were up, we extended the arrangement for six months, t. Then for a year. Now we don't even bother talking about ending it. We know how well it works and wish we had settled on it even before we married.

Whichever of us has erred, is punished to a degree appropriate to the lapse. For example, although my wife knows she needs to keep "To–do" lists and work from them, she sometimes forgets to do errands, like making a bank deposit or picking up dry cleaning. That draws 15 to 20 spanks, depending on how important the task was. Another constant problem is that my wife takes so long to get dressed when we are going out that we often arrive at the event late. Unexcused tardiness (for either of us) merits 25 spanks.

We worked out a list of faults and corresponding punishments, which we often discuss and revise. Nine times out of ten, the guilty party admits the fault and therefore must accept the punishment.

For instance, a few days ago my wife took an eternity to get dressed and put on her makeup, and we arrived late to an important business dinner, a lapse not good for my career. She knew what was in store for her when we got home, and asked to be punished.

As many other couples do, at least judging from your letters, we have a ritual or ceremony we go through each time. We followed it when we came home from the dinner.

I didn't even have my wife change out of her tiny cocktail dress first. She stood in front of me and raised her dress to her hips. I pulled her panties down to her knees. I asked her whether she had been at fault, and she said "Yes." I asked her whether she accepted her punishment as fair, and she said "Yes."

I gave my wife the choice of being spanked with my hand, her hairbrush, our sawed–off bath brush, or our ping pong paddle. She chose the hairbrush, fetched it and handed it to me with downcast eyes. She could have chosen my hand, a much lighter punishment, but she knew she had messed up and wanted a severe blistering.

I whacked my wife with the hairbrush 25 times. She was crying like a baby long before I finished, though she did not beg me to stop. Not that crying or begging helps. Our rule is that once the punishment is decided on, it *must* be carried out in full, and crying and pleading must be ignored.

When I was finished, I rubbed my wife's bottom, praised her for taking her punishment well, then sent her to stand in the corner for ten minutes. That's the last part of the punishment, the final step in the ritual.

When it is my turn to be punished the ritual is slightly different. Since I am a man, she secures me. I am much stronger than her and this avoids the possibility that in my pain and frustration, I might get up and stop the punishment. She strips me and puts me on the bed or sofa, face down. She ties my hands with an old necktie and whips my bottom with a leather belt.

My wife uses her full strength to strap me fifteen to twenty–five times, and I always end up in tears just as she does.

I know our system of insuring domestic harmony is not common. But we both firmly feel that our system of spankings has helped our marriage. I want to make clear that these punishments are enough to get the message across, but are not brutal or damaging. When I spank my wife, any real pain and redness are usually gone within a day; when I am strapped, within two days. We do not mark each other and would stop the moment we saw that happening. (One reason, by the way, along with the humiliation and sexiness, that every punishment is on the bare behind.)

It is reassuring to know that our system may be unusual, but there are other couples with similar methods. In fact, we are close friends with a married couple who do the same thing. That's where my wife got the idea of a punishment agreement in the first place. She told her girlfriend about our situation and her girlfriend said, "Why don't you try what my husband and I do?" That is how my wife happened to bring up the idea out of the blue.

My wife and I have nothing in our backgrounds that might have contributed to our love of spanking for punishment and as an erotic turn–on. I can't remember anything unusual, or any spanking that got me excited; I hated every one I got. My wife hated her childhood spankings, but did have one interesting experience as a teenager that she remembers. Here's what she says:

"I was never spanked as a small girl. I got my first spanking at the advanced age of 16 when my mother died (my father already had) and I had to go live with an older sister and her husband.

Soon after moving in with them, we started to have arguments, mostly about my dating behavior. In addition, I was uncomfortable because my brother–in–law seemed to show more interest in me than he should have. One evening I returned from a date quite late at night. Or, I should say, quite early in the morning. In addition, it was a school night. And my lipstick and makeup were smudged. And I had wine on my breath. And I had a hickey. My brother–in–law was angry and insisted to my sister I should be punished on the spot.

My sister agreed and sent me to her bedroom to get a hairbrush. As I gave it to her I was afraid of what was about to happen, yet I had a weird excited feeling, especially *there.*

My sister sat down on the couch, and in front of her husband raised my skirt, lowered my panties to my ankles, then put me across her lap. I was even more *tingly* in that position, fearful and curious about the spanking, but embarrassed at my brother–in–law seeing me nude. All my feelings were mixed together.

My sister gave me a terrific walloping with that nasty hairbrush. She must have spanked me about thirty times. Although it was terribly painful and I cried throughout the spanking and for awhile after, I was weirdly excited from the sting and pain as the hairbrush whacked me again and again.

To be honest, when I thought about it afterward, I was also excited by my brother–in–law watching me get spanked and seeing all my girl parts, since he stood right behind me the whole time for a perfect view. While I was being spanked, I resented him taking advantage of the situation; even if my sister were going to spank me, since she was my guardian, he had no right to a closeup view. But afterward, thinking about the show I was giving him as my behind turned red, gave me strange feelings.

When my sister finished paddling me, she ordered me to stand in a corner like a little girl, holding up my skirt with both hands so I couldn't rub myself, and with my panties at my ankles. While I stood there humiliated and crying, she and her husband lectured me about my dating behavior. When I looked at myself in a mirror afterward, I was shocked by how my behind was covered with angry burning red blotches. It hurt for half a day, then itched maddeningly for another day.

That wasn't the first time my sister paddled me with her hairbrush. I got punished about every three weeks, and my brother–in–law watched every spanking. I'm sure he would have loved to strip me himself and put me over his knee, and I'm still not quite sure how I would have felt about that. Let's just say I would have had mixed feelings.

I guess this experience — of being spanked for the first time at age 16 by my sister rather than a parent, and spanked bare in front of my brother–in–law, makes my spanking history a little different from most. Maybe it got spanking mixed up with feelings I now recognize as powerfully sexual. Anyhow, I agree with my husband that our spankings have done a great deal for our marriage. They encourage good and loving behavior, and improve our sex life by getting us both very excited. What more could we ask?"

x x x

TEENAGE SPANKINGS LEAD TO LOVE

— JUDITH A., CHICAGO, ILLINOIS

I have been fascinated by your contributors' different experiences and attitudes toward spanking. Some report no sexual element whatsoever; just pain and humiliation, especially when the punishment is on the nude buttocks and in an especially exposing posture. Some of these even accuse the ones who enjoy spanking of being strange or abnormal.

Others explain in a quite matter–of–fact way that spanking is a big part of their sex lives, that it gets them excited, that they use it as foreplay to sex or even as a "main dish" in itself. These enthusiasts, in their turn, may accuse their critics of being unworldly, boring, hypocritical or afraid of exploring their own sexuality.

I don't think there's some single Truth. I believe everyone is "wired" differently, perhaps even physically different in their sexual parts, and what is only painful to some, is pleasurably painful to others. In addition, being bared and exposed can be only humiliating to some, but the humiliation is sexually exciting to others.

I think some people, and not others, have a spanking gene. It may be switched on at an early age. It may be switched on in adolescence from either parental punishment or sexual experimentation between boys and girls. Birthday spankings, anyone? For late bloomers, it may be switched on even in the twenties.

But some unfortunate people deny their feelings and deny themselves what could give them enormous pleasure.

Enough philosophizing. As far as myself, I am a twenty–six–year–old woman. I grew up in a small town in Iowa but now live in Chicago. I was spanked a few times as a child, only for extreme misbehavior, and got zero pleasure out of those spankings. I dreaded my mother's hairbrush and my father's hard hand. These spankings continued until I was twelve and started developing.

When I was fourteen, though, my spanking gene got switched on. I can tell you the exact day and hour — June 18, 8:15 p.m. After my 14th birthday party, my boyfriend and I found ourselves alone, and he insisted on giving me a private birthday spanking. It started off innocent — just his hand over my panties, and hardly more than love pats. But on an impulse I challenged him to give me a *real* spanking. He was nervous at first, but I told him if he didn't do it right, I'd tell everyone at school he was chicken.

When my boyfriend started spanking me for real, I got so excited I was writhing around on his lap and he was frightened(!) I begged him to spank me even harder. When he'd given me 14, I told him it was supposed to be 14 on *each* side, and made him give me another 14 with my hairbrush. My panties never came down that time — I didn't want to give the poor boy a heart attack — but he did get his hands under my panties and fondle me as I had orgasm after orgasm. Then I insisted on another few hairbrush spanks for luck and fortune. My behind was in agony and I was in ecstasy. I made him pull my panty sides together into my butt crack to expose my behind, and we were both astonished by the heat and color from the spanking.

After that, I got my boyfriend to spank me as often as we could find privacy. It wasn't always easy to arrange as we were only 14. But we took long nature hikes together, and he had an older brother whose apartment we could borrow sometimes. Most of the year we had to do it on Friday evenings or weekends, to allow my behind time to recover and not go to school Monday in a condition that would raise questions.

Soon after that birthday spanking we graduated to him spanking me on the bare. We'd start with his hand, then use the hairbrush. Sometimes I'd be over his lap for half an hour while he took turns spanking me and fondling me like crazy to orgasm after orgasm. He even learned to insert his lubricated finger in my rear and work it around while I shuddered and bucked. Not something that every 14–year–old girl goes for, but I loved it. By the time I finally got around to losing my virginity with him, on my 16th birthday, he'd spanked me dozens and dozens of times. After my 16th birthday, we had sex all the time. Sodomy too. My parents knew about the sex, but we never told anyone about all the spanking or the sodomy. They wouldn't have wanted to know.

And by the way, he is the only boyfriend I've ever had, or wanted. We were perfectly suited for each other, perfect fits sexually, work in the same field, and even have the same taste in music, art and politics. We have been in love and been spanking partners since we were 14, lovers since we were 16, and married since we were 19. And I still love being put over his knee and feeling a firm hand or a hard oak hairbrush warming me up.

x x x

MY BIGGEST SPANKING THRILL

— R. J., KENTUCKY

My biggest thrill from a spanking wasn't from one I got or gave, and there have been many of those over the years. It was from one I watched.

I was thirteen and a half at the time it happened. I was no stranger to corporal punishment. When I was caught being disobedient or mouthy I was turned over my mother's knee, where I got my bottom warmed by her firm hand. I was allowed panties if the fault was small, but usually bare bottom. Either way, the spankings weren't fun or exciting, and certainly not *sexually* exciting, even when I reached puberty. They were just *painful*. Painful to anticipate, painful to receive, painful afterward.

One late afternoon as I was coming toward the house, I saw my older brother, who was then 16, being taken toward the woodshed by my father. From their body language and expressions I knew something was up and sure enough I wanted to see whatever it was.

I made sure they didn't see me. Hiding behind shrubbery, I got to the far side of the woodshed and climbed an outside ladder where I could see in through a high window. I wasn't allowed up there and was risking dire punishment myself.

By the time I reached my spy nest, my brother had his pants and underwear down and was turned with his back toward away from me. There was a saddle on a stand, and my brother was lying over it with his bottom toward me and jutting up. Dad had a paddle and whacked him with it again and again. He must have paddled him about ten times. My brother's bottom was bright red all over. I couldn't hear him crying but his whole body shuddered with each paddle stroke. His buttocks would get flattened and then bounce back and jiggle for a moment. Then my father would give him the next one.

The paddling didn't end my brother's punishment. My father got a long riding crop and whipped him with that. Where my brother's bottom had been bright red, now it was bright red with thin redder lines crossing both cheeks and the top of his thighs, and especially where the cheeks meet the thighs.

My brother lay limp over the saddle until my father grabbed him by the neck and yanked him to his feet. Then he stood there with tears rolling down his cheeks, holding his bottom cheeks with both hands. I could see his penis and balls, too, and he had an *erection* to which my father paid no attention. My father told him to stand in the corner and come in the house when he'd stopped crying. He went in the corner and stood there a long time feeling his ravaged behind and masturbating himself till he spurted all over the straw.

I was incredibly, unbelievably, amazingly excited seeing the whole scene. Much more excited than the few times when I'd French kissed boys or let them feel my breasts, which was as far as I'd gone till then. I managed to get down the side of the shed without being spotted and wandered into the house as if nothing had happened.

"Where did you go, Pumpkin?"

"Out."

"What did you do?"

"Nothing. Is there time for me to shower before dinner?"

Of course I wanted to shower. I was still so excited I was afraid my parents would *smell* my excitement on me. In the shower, I masturbated like crazy.

From then on, I constantly wondered what a severe punishment like that would feel like. How would I feel when I knew I was going to be punished? Would I have the same pain my brother felt, or were girls different from boys? The same pleasure I had from watching, mixed with the pain? What would it feel like afterward? How long till the pain went away? The welts?

Unfortunately, no matter how much I provoked them, the most I ever got was over–the–knee spankings from my mother. I did "graduate" from mostly panties to always getting them bare bottom; and my mother did upgrade to a big mean hairbrush rather than her hand. So by the time she got through with me, I'd be thoroughly red and sore. I tried to get myself paddled as often as possible, which for a while was about once a week until I sensed my parents starting to wonder. But certainly those hairbrush paddlings were *nothing* like what I had seen my brother get. I wanted a *burning, blistered* bottom and welts that would last for days.

My brother and I were close, and I asked him a million questions about his punishment, but he didn't want to talk about it. I finally swore him to secrecy and confessed what I wanted. He was willing but afraid. He said if our parents ever found out, they'd skin both our butts with a whip.

"Fine with me," I said. But he still wouldn't. We would have had to be alone for a few days so he could really punish me like I wanted and I'd have time to recover my usual butt color in case anyone got a glimpse or became suspicious. But somehow we never managed it.

When I started really dating, I very carefully hinted around the subject to a few boys, but they thought people who wanted to be spanked were touched and spanking was only for punishment, so I was afraid to push things farther. Then I ended up getting married straight out of high school. My husband is great, treats me like a queen, provides well, but is absolutely straight sexually. No interest at all in spanking. And I'd consider going and getting spanked, even by a professional, to be cheating on him, which I wouldn't do.

So there I am. Who was it who said so wisely, "We shouldn't regret the things we do, we should regret the things we didn't do?"

x x x

WHACKING HIS GIRLFRIEND TURNS HER ON

— RONALD T., ILLINOIS

I'm in my early 30's, make a good living in a government job, have a masters degree, enjoy outdoor sports and indoor games, am reasonably good looking, normal in all respects, and engaged to a beautiful girl I have known for years. She's 24. We both enjoy spanking sessions very much.

If one actually looks into the matter, it is obvious that spanking is far more widespread than most people realize. And spanking is used for many reasons: true discipline, sexual excitement, to express dominance and submission or even mastership and slavery, sometimes several things together.

However, what almost all accounts have in common is that the person being spanked is bare bottom. Most of the men and women refer to their spankings being on their naked buttocks. To me this means that sexual excitement is the key motivation, even where the participants claim the spanking is for other reasons. I know that many women write in that their husbands or boyfriends spank them only for disciplinary reasons, and the nudity is only to make the pain worse or to enhance the punishment with embarrassment. Teenage boys and girls say the same thing about bare bottom punishments at the hands of their parents.

I take these protestations with a grain of salt. There's nothing sexier than a bare female bottom. Especially a bare female bottom bent over a piece of furniture or your lap, positions that reveal the woman's sexual parts and anus.

I don't remember when I got the notion that it would be great fun to spank girls, but certainly before I reached junior high school. Quite a few western movies included scenes where the bratty cowgirl, daughter, bride–to–be or young wife got a thorough spanking, though sadly they never showed nudity. I remember getting wildly excited at these scenes. I had lost interest in cowboy movies by thirteen, so certainly the notion of spanking got me excited long before puberty. Long before I even knew much about what sex was.

In high school all the girls talked about everything with each other. I certainly tried to sleep with any girl I went out with, or at least get as far as I could. Remember 1st base, 2nd base, etc.? But I didn't dare suggest putting them over my lap for a butt warming, or it would have been all over the school and then the town. I might as well have run an announcement in the weekly. You can imagine what the people at my church would have said about me propositioning some adolescent virgin for a spanking. Had I actually gotten lucky and spanked her, it would have been even worse, even though most of the parents probably spanked or used the switch on their teenage daughters and enjoyed it.

My first steady who really meant anything to me, was a girl I met at the start of my last year of high school. Susan was a real stunner, with a beautiful face, black hair, green eyes and milky skin (she stayed out of the sun, unlike most of the girls who loved the outdoors). She had the world's most perfect butt. Even today, looking at old snapshots, I shake my head. The boys called her Susie Bubble Butt. I couldn't keep my hands off her, especially her butt, when we were alone. We really steamed up my car at the drive–ins.

After we'd been going out a few months I summoned my courage and got around to the subject of spanking. She was *absolutely* not interested. I brought up the subject several times in a nice way and found out she'd been subjected to many spankings as a child and was still getting spanked as a senior in high school.

She didn't want to talk about it but I wormed some of the details out of her. When she was younger her mother was the one who punished her, first with the hand, later with a little souvenir paddle from Yosemite National Park. On one side it said "Heat for the Seat" with a cartoon of a girl being paddled; it had a picture of Half Dome on the flip side. Susan was spanked bare over the lap. Not just with her clothes and panties down at her knees, but starkers. "Not a stitch." Susan hated these punishments, especially because her parents let her bratty little brother watch and tease her.

When Susan reached her teens, her father took over punishment duties. He used the paddle too, but spanked harder and longer than Susan's mom had. But she was still starkers, over his lap, with the brat watching and teasing her. After the spanking, she'd have to stand in the corner with her hands behind her head for ten minutes while the brat stood behind her, telling her how red her butt was and asking whether it smarted.

This all came out in a rush one night after we'd been drinking wine. I guess she wanted to get it off her chest (which was beautiful, by the way, medium sized, very firm breasts, with large nipples that stood out like bullets the moment you petted them). Then she clammed up. I filled in some details from the brat, too. All it took was bribing him with milk shakes and candy bars and helping him with his baseball fielding. Also I'd found out about some vandalism he and his friends had gotten up to, and I told him he could tell me *everything* about Susan's spankings, or I'd tell his parents who was blowing up the town's mailboxes with cherry bombs and M–80's.

Susan loved her parents dearly but bitterly resented these punishments. Not just the pain, especially with her dad spanking her, but the humiliation. "I'm angry and frustrated every time I think of it," she told me.

We eventually broke up for reasons having nothing to do with my spanking interest, but are still in touch. I don't think she remembers my spanking interest and my attempts to talk her into being spanked. She's still the prettiest and sexiest woman I've ever met, and has the best butt I've ever laid my hand on, although I'd never tell that to my present girlfriend.

That girlfriend — we're really "engaged to be engaged" — is different in her attitudes. She'd been spanked as a child but the spankings were mild and ended when she reached adolescence at 12½.

"My dad had spanked the hell out of me with his hand. I felt like I'd sat on a hot stove. I was standing there in the corner with my pants and everything at my ankles like usual and overheard them talking. My dad told my mom, 'I think Claire's getting a little too old for spankings. She's getting breasts and a muff, for Chrissakes. I don't want to turn her into a perv, for Chrissakes.' They talked about it a long time. Whether mom should do the spanking instead, or dad should keep doing it but let me keep panties on, and blah, blah. But finally they agreed I was too old. After that it was groundings and taking away phone privileges and other things. I hated that. I would have rather be spanked. At least it's over fast."

Still, when we first began seeing each other, Claire had never even heard of people spanking each other for sexual pleasure. Her first reaction to my hints was "no," but it was a tentative, thoughtful "no." After awhile she came around, agreeing that it was worth a try. I promised if she tried it three times, different ways and didn't enjoy it, I wouldn't press her.

I had the feeling that in the back of her mind Claire may have enjoyed the spankings from her parents, and generally liked being submissive. Unlike Susan, Claire loved talking about her spankings, her feelings, how her butt felt, all the details. But few women will come right out and admit they want a spanking as much as you want to give them one; they have to *reluctantly* let you *persuade* them to try it.

At the beginning I didn't spank Claire very hard, and she kept her dress or slacks on. I told her it was ridiculous and I could hardly aim, and suggested her dress be pinned out of the way. She knew she had great legs and agreed to that, and I enjoyed the view of her panty–covered butt. Especially on hot days or after we'd worked up a sweat dancing, when her panties would cling to her butt crack and half the butt would be exposed.

After I'd spanked her a number of times, the final step was

lowering her panties. As usual, she didn't just come out and say, "Pull 'em down, cowboy!" No, we had to play the game. I told her it was a *safety* measure. I wanted to be able to aim, see her butt and make sure I wasn't hitting her too hard, blah, blah, blah. It was all B.S. but I said it with a straight face.

"I guess that makes sense," she said. "You're sure you're just looking out for me, right?"

I knew she was enjoying the spankings. She was letting me spank her more and more often. She wasn't objecting when I spanked her harder and longer. Also, her excitement was obvious, and the harder I spanked the more excited she got. She was leaving damp spots on my chinos, for heaven's sakes. Maybe she was timid about baring all or maybe she felt she had to put on a show of reluctance so I wouldn't think she was easy. But after convincing her it would be not only safer, but more fun for both of us, and endlessly praising her butt, the panties came down too on one glorious evening.

Honestly the first time this happened, I was more nervous than she was. She was over my lap and raised up an inch so I could pull her panties down to her knees. She lay there, utterly submissive. I was so nervous I could hardly speak, and my heart was thumping. But once I started spanking, my jitters went away.

It was *so* much more fun than spanking her over panties. There was the warmth under my hand. There was the view. She didn't object as I gently pried her legs apart so I could spank the inside parts of her cheeks — and open that view. What a wonderful sight to see her butt cheeks, liberated from those silly panties, bouncing under each spank and quickly reddening.

She gasped and cried out with some of the spanks, especially toward the end, but her arousal couldn't have been more obvious, and even though she sobbing, she never asked to stop. I paused often to caress her cheeks, praise her beauty and tell her how well she was taking her spanking.

That first time broke the ice and all the spankings after that were bare butt. Sometimes with clothes pulled down to make a confining rope around her ankles or knees — symbolic bondage? Sometimes I didn't allow her a stitch. We were both completely at ease with the spankings and she loved every session as I did, and encouraged more and more painful spankings. Usually we had sex afterward, or at least she gave me a blow job, another activity that took a period of persuasion, even though I know she was eager for it for a long time. We've been together for almost a year now.

After much experimentation, we have settled on quantity rather than quality for a number of reasons. First, she doesn't want to be damaged. A hundred moderate hand spanks are safer than thirty hard ones or fifteen with a hairbrush.

Second, there are no lasting effects. She can take many moderate hand spanks. Her butt will be hot and she'll be totally turned on, but the soreness and color will disappear fast. She's always good to go, ready for more spanking the next day. Well, two days anyhow.

Third, the spanking itself is almost secondary to the whole ritual surrounding it. There's the warning beforehand. Making her stand in front of me. Me sitting, she submissive and standing, while I slowly remove her clothes. Pulling down her panties is a step I draw out, lowering them and teasingly, with lots of praise for her beautiful beaver and butt. Then there's the ritual of putting her over my knee with endless adjusting. I use the opportunity to feel her everywhere, so she's usually breathing hard before I even start the spanking.

Fourth, the longer the spanking lasts, the more fun we both have, and the more it emphasizes her submission and my mastery.

Anyway, we've tried a lot of things and this is what we settled on. It's an incredible turn on for both of us, and we intend to keep up the spanking after we are married.

We've tried using implements such as paddles, rulers, belts and hairbrushes, but she prefers feeling my hand spanking her. She says, "I don't want to feel a piece of wood or leather, I want to feel your hand." She likes being spanked all over the butt, but there are two areas that are special to her. One is the crease where the butt meets the legs. The other is the inside of the butt cheeks. This requires her spreading her legs and really bending over so her butt juts up and opens. I also may have to pull the far cheek out of the way to blister the inside of the near cheek. Then I have to turn her the other way over my knee to work her other cheek with my left hand and make them a match. I've seen photos of spanked women in men's magazines and wonder why no one makes an effort to spank the inside of the cheeks. It's so sensitive and so close to the prettiest spots on a woman's body.

That is our story. I am lucky to have found a woman who shares my interest. Like I say, I don't think I really guided her into it; the interest was always there and she just needed a way to safely admit it. I don't think I'll every get tired of spanking a woman.

One side note: my girlfriend also has a bratty, bitchy side at times. She knows that if she misbehaves during our marriage, I will take her over my knee for a hard paddling, a real punishment paddling with nothing sexy about it, and me using a hairbrush if I see fit. Or even bending her over a sofa arm and employing a strap, cane or switch. We've discussed that several times and she says she will accept such loving discipline. When we take our marriage vows, they will be the traditional ones where the wife promises to *obey* her husband. I'm sure the prospect of domestic corporal punishment, like the sexual spankings, will enhance our marriage.

X X X

SPANKED AS A SORORITY PLEDGE, SPANKED BY HER BOSS

— MARGIE T., TACOMA, WASHINGTON

I am a tax paralegal in an accounting firm, 27, still single, considered very attractive — and get a huge amount of pleasure from being spanked.

I am the younger of two girls. My parents were very loving and never spanked either of us. Really, they spoiled us if anything. I've been very curious about my love for spanking ever since I recognized it in myself long before puberty. But I didn't connect it to *sex* until much later. I have done quite a bit of reading on the subject and some psychological self–analysis. At first I lacked the means to get professional help. Later I had the means but was to embarrassed to discuss an interest that I considered abnormal. Finally I came to accept my interest and decided I didn't need any professional help.

I was a late bloomer sexually and my first awareness that the mention or thought of spanking stimulated a sensation *there* came when I was just short of 15 years old. I had several close girlfriends who would share their stories of physical punishment by their parents and I would try to draw out all the details: what did everyone say beforehand, were my friends allowed to keep their panties on, who did the punishing, were both parents there, were brothers and sisters allowed to watch, what did the

77

parent use, what posture did they put the girl in, how hard did they spank, how many times, did they spank rapidly or draw it out, how did the spanking feel (especially, how did it feel!), how long did it take, did the girl have to stand in a corner before or after, did her siblings tease her, how did her behind feel afterward, what did it look like, how long did it hurt, did she resent her parents for the punishment, and every other detail.

We also had long discussions about whether it was better to be spanked, even severely, or be punished by grounding, chores, phone privileges taken away, and so on. My friends were split 50/50 whether they preferred to be spanked or punished in other ways. I, unfortunately, was never spanked, so I couldn't judge.

Several of my friends were also punished by having their mouths washed out with soap, especially for bad language or back talk, and they hated that worse than spanking. Washing kids' mouths out with soap was rare even then, but no one considered it "abusive."

I had two girlfriends who received punishment *enemas*, a word I didn't even know until they explained, and I was horrified and fascinated at the same time. Again, a rare punishment, but I don't think most people considered it abusive. Getting my mouth washed out with soap and getting punishment enemas are experiences I've never chosen to explore!

Spanking, however, fascinated me. I became a real expert on all the methods parents used to punish their teenage boys and (more often) girls. Among my friends' parents the most popular tools were bare hand and hairbrush. Trailing in popularity were the strap or belt, the ping pong paddle and the switch. Everything else was a distant also–ran.

Speaking of the switch, practically every house had a tree or bush suitable for cutting switches. If it didn't, the parent would send their child next door to ask the neighbor for permission to cut a switch for her own punishment. You can imagine the hilarity and teasing if the neighbor's children heard the request.

I had no interest in spanking of pre–adolescent children; I just felt sorry for them. When my friends would start talking about their much younger brothers and sisters, I would tune out until we got back on *my* topic. It was spanking of adolescents, or almost–adolescents, that got me excited.

I liked hearing about spankings given by the father or other male relative such as uncle or grandfather, rather than the mother. One girl had a widowed mother. Her mother considered herself too weak to do a good spanking, so the girl was regularly over her *brother's* lap for bare bottom spankings, even though her brother was only two years older. Her descriptions of those spankings got me so excited I was almost dizzy.

My sensations were greatest when I heard about a girl being punished bare bottom, and severely. I found it very hard to conceal my excitement as I feasted on all the details. Good thing I was a girl; if I'd been a boy I would have had a tent in my pants.

Even in their teens, most of my spanked girlfriends had their panties lowered for punishment. Surprisingly, they didn't mind telling all the exciting details. Three of them would even drop their panties to let me and others see how red their bottom was after a session with their parent's hairbrush or strap. It was fascinating to see the color and feel the heat. I still carry the pictures in my mind, and I can still feel the warmth in their cupped behinds. Thank you, Laura, Kim, and Dawn, wherever you are.

My biggest thrill of those years came when I actually saw a spanking for the first time, rather than just heard about one. I was sixteen and staying at a girlfriend's lake house for a three day weekend. We went to a party and staggered back blasted in the wee hours.

My friend's mother was waiting for us. With hardly a word, she laid her daughter over her knee, pulled up her dress and pinned it out of the way with two clothespins, and ordered her to raise up so she could pull down her panties. Then the mom laid into my friend with a big hairbrush.

From the way my friend screamed with each hairbrush spank, cried and begged, it was obvious the spanking was really stinging her. Her mom kept it up quite a long time and I was very excited watching my friend's creamy buttocks turn pink, then hot pink, then red, then deep red, with hairbrush–shaped blotches down to the top of the thighs.

Her mother gave me a lecture too and threatened me with a dose of the same medicine, but to my disappointment she didn't. If only she had ordered me over her lap, I would have leaped into place. But she wasn't going to call my parents for permission to spank me at 2 a.m., and she let it slide. My friend cried for a long time after that punishment, probably as much from the humiliation in front of me as from the pain. We were sharing the same bed, and I kept running my hand over her burning buttocks to comfort her until I started to worry what she might think.

I got my first real spanking at my college sorority. During the initiation all the freshmen pledges were paddled several times, but unfortunately only over skirts or pants. I would have liked to see their bare bottoms turning red under those oak weapons.

Whenever we were ordered to "assume the position," the other girls moaned and whined. I enjoyed my paddlings, though. There was one other girl in my pledge class who felt the same way I did. We never spoke about it, both of us pretended to hate being paddled, but I could *tell*. When you have a special interest, sometimes your antenna sense like–minded folks even across a room. It reminds me of a homosexual boy I knew, who told me boys like him can spot each other.

My sorority Big Sister, a senior, must have enjoyed paddling girls. When she had an excuse, she'd order me to bring the paddle. Then I'd be told to "assume the position" for breaking one of the countless rules that tripped up new members. Usually she would paddle me when I was in pyjamas or nightie, or she'd lift my skirt and paddle me on the panties, three to five times, a real punishment with that heavy oak paddle. Although the swats were shockingly painful, I loved them.

We freshmen were required to report our own misdeeds, so I was sometimes able to get myself paddled without making everyone suspicious I was a glutton for punishment. But my Big Sister knew.

I cherished those paddlings. They would have been better only if they were more frequent, more severe, on my perfect bare bottom, administered by a boy and photographed and filmed for posterity.

I really wanted to get it bare bottom, however. So one day when I was supposed to do something important — buy sup-plies for a fund–raising car wash — I deliberately forgot to buy the stuff, and when my Big Sister cornered me I said I didn't think it was that important and I'd do it later.

As I'd planned, I was ordered to fetch the paddle and assume the position, which meant leaning over and holding my ankles with legs shoulder width apart. When my Big Sister lifted my skirt, she was surprised by the view of my bare buttocks and, in that position, everything else I had. Yes, I had left them off. That was a blatant violation of our house's "Rules of Dress and Deportment."

I got what I'd been looking for, the most severe paddling yet, and on the bare. And I loved it, just as I knew I would. The pain, embarrassment and submission all mixed in together to make a potent brew that had me delirious with pleasure.

My Big Sister must have enjoyed the bare bottom paddling, too, because after that session she would punish me privately and always make me drop everything first.

Getting a boy to spank me was trickier because I was rather shy with them, and afraid to ask for what I wanted. In addition, I was afraid that if I let a boy spank me, let alone asked for a spanking, the word would get out that I was "odd." Having sex wouldn't ruin a girl's rep. Neither would giving blow jobs. But anything offbeat like wanting to be spanked or be tied up, would. I never did get spanked by a boy at college, except for a playful birthday spanking where I got passed around from boy to boy at our linked fraternity. Just for fun, fully clothed, and non–pain-ful, more's the pity.

When I graduated college and started my career, I decided I was finally going to get a proper spanking. And the lucky man I chose was my own boss. He was very nice, about my own fa-ther's age, even looked a little like my father (!) He was married with grown children. I'd had dinner with him and his wife, and somehow it had come out that he and his wife had spanked their children, even as teenagers. Interesting. I thought I also saw a gleam in my boss's eye when he looked at me sometimes.

One day at work I messed up a document badly and my boss joked that I knew better and deserved a spanking for a screw–up like that. Even though I knew he was just kidding, I had to leave his office at once because I blushed and felt myself starting to get tingly.

A few times after that he made similar remarks with the same result.

About six months into my job, my boss mentioned that his wife was going out of town and that he'd be spending the whole weekend to catch up on work and fix up his office (finally hang artwork, diplomas and professional membership certificates, etc.) I offered to help with the office decorating.

On Saturday afternoon the place was empty. Even the cleaning lady was gone by noon. We'd hung all the stuff and his office looked like a million bucks. Before we quit and left, I told him I wanted to talk to him about something but it was "half business and half personal, so I was a little uncomfortable." I'd rehearsed my approach for a week, ever since he'd mentioned coming in on the weekend.

"You can talk to me about anything," my boss said. "The worst that can happen is I'll put it in the company newsletter." Ha, ha.

I told my boss I'd been thinking about what he said about my work on the "Smith Project" and he was right.

He said he didn't remember what he'd said. I reminded him that he'd said I should be spanked when I messed up.

He was embarrassed and said he'd just been joking. But I wasn't going to be denied that easily. I said I'd thought he was right at the time; my error could have cost the firm thousands of dollars and punishment was appropriate. I reminded him that he and his wife had spanked their children, even as teenagers. I persuaded him that I deserved a spanking.

I said I realized the request made him feel uncomfortable, but it would be a kindness to me because it would improve my work attitude and help my career. Wasn't guidance like that part of his job? Etc. etc. I'd practiced my whole little speech in front of my mirror at home.

I could see my boss was eager, but afraid of doing something so totally inappropriate at work. Still, he agreed. I quickly pulled down my slacks and laid myself across his lap before he could change his mind. He gave me about twenty good hard spanks with his hand. They stung well, got me very excited, and I could see and *feel* he was excited too. In fact, right after the spanking he excused himself to go to the bathroom.

My boss took me out to dinner that night, and in our secluded corner booth, we had a nice talk about spanking, in which I did most of the talking and he listened intently. I knew plenty about spanking (having learned it all from my friends) but made up stories about being spanked over my father's knee. I also made up some whoppers about my first office job when I was fifteen, claiming I'd had a boss who spanked me bare bottom when I made mistakes at work, and it did me good. Completely untrue, but the man had passed away, so there was no way for my boss to even check.

My boss accepted my invitation for a drink at my apartment. As he was drinking his brandy, I opened my purse, pulled out a hairbrush, made a show of inspecting it and placed it meaningfully on the end table in front of him.

"I should keep one of these around the office," he said.

" 'Be prepared' is the Boy Scout motto," I said with a demure smile. (He was a scoutmaster.) "But why don't you finish the job now?"

He didn't need much persuasion. He pulled me over his lap and got my pants down.

I raised up and he accepted that invitation to ruck down my panties.

He did a great job. He set my poor buttocks on fire with that hairbrush, smacking every spot again and again. Not only the main parts, but especially the super–sensitive bottom areas where the buttock cheeks meet the thighs. I don't know which was louder; the smacking sound of the hairbrush or my crying. I think he was nervous he was punishing me too hard, but I never asked him to stop, just lay there crying and shaking. With that hairbrush spanking I was releasing years of pent–up desire and I didn't want it to end.

When he finished, he said, "I was afraid I was spanking you too hard. You're sure you're okay? Do you know what your bottom looks like?"

"No, but I know what it feels like," I said.

I lay on my tummy on my bed and he massaged cold cream into my buttocks. I don't think it eased the pain much, but it felt great to have him squeezing and kneading my ravaged behind. I would have enjoyed having him take me any way he wanted, but I liked his wife too much and he was faithful to her also.

As he was leaving, he said again, "I hope I wasn't too hard on you." I put my finger to his lips to stop the nonsense and gave him a big hug.

I don't work for that firm any more, but my old boss still offers me spanking relief at least every two weeks, sometimes more often. He thinks of me almost as another daughter. He loves that I talk to him about my achievements and problems. We have lunch or dinner every month or two.

My old boss loves to sail. He takes me out on his sailboat now and then, and there's nothing like being spanked on a bare bottom soaked with salt water. It hurts twice as much but doesn't do any more damage; what more can a girl ask?

Sometimes, if the weather is warm and there aren't other boats around, I'll spend the whole cruise naked except for a life vest. He'll make me bend over and whip me with a cane or rope length, just like they did to boy sailors in the Age of Sail. Wetted down first, of course. I end up with spectacular burning welts. I've declined a cat–o'–nine–tails, though. I don't even know where you'd buy one these days.

It's comforting to know that whenever I get the urge to be spanked, I can call up my old boss and he'll relieve my need. I'll say I've messed up at work, or treated someone poorly, or let my apartment go to seed. Or I'll just say, "I think I need some guidance."

He still spanks me with the hairbrush, and I love the warmth and security of being over his lap. But we also try other things. I have a rattan cane from England, a long riding crop, and a plastic cane and paddle which can be used only in moderation, even for me. Our favorite is an old fashioned brown razor strap, shortened to about a foot plus the handle. He gave it to me as a Christmas present. I am required to keep it well oiled and supple, and honestly I can get excited just rubbing it down with mink oil. No nine–year–old with his first baseball glove ever treated his tool of trade with more loving care. Sometimes if I know I'll be punished with it the next day, I sleep with it under my pillow.

My old boss always bares my bottom for my spankings, and sometimes bares all of me. My clothing, if any, my posture and the severity of my spanking are up to him; he should know by now what's best for me! Sometimes I'll request a particular implement, but the choice — or choices — are always up to him. He's in charge.

Despite the fact that my parts are visible, especially when I'm bent over with legs spread, he has never made a pass at me. The closest he'll come is squeezing my buttocks during and after the spanking. How many men could resist making a pass, with the sight of a young woman's bright red, hot, trembling buttocks, with her flower and button staring at them and begging for attention? But he's a gentleman. He certainly enjoys his role, though, and gives me a good blistering every time.

Spanking me seems to have turned him on to spanking, and he's started spanking his wife. He gives me blow–by–blow accounts, and they get me excited even before he turns his hand to me. His wife doesn't like being spanked, though. Or at least that's what she tells him.

Although my need to be spanked is certainly driven by sexual desires, it is a separate thing. I enjoy sex in all its versions — regular intercourse, oral, even anal — but I never have sex with the men who spank me or vice–versa. I think that's unusual.

I have been spanked by many men, but just as one night stands or a few times. Sometimes the man will want sex but I can divert him into spanking me instead, which is good for me but less than satisfying for them. Very few are good at spanking me the first time. They're nervous, afraid to take my panties down, afraid to spank me hard, and afraid to use a hairbrush or anything else. Then they want to stop the spanking the moment they see me reddening up. They're confused and afraid to continue just when I am sexually excited the most, despite all my crying. Maybe they're threatened by seeing me so aroused.

Only one of my dates proved skillful at the first go. When we came back to my apartment I invited him in for a drink. He had ideas but I teased him into spanking me instead. It was a pleasant surprise when, unlike the others, he took control. He ordered me to take my dress off, and then my panties. Then he ordered me to take everything off. Then he ordered me to find a hairbrush.

I offered him the hairbrush, but he said, "Present it properly." Playing along, I curtsied, got on my knees and presented it to him with both hands. Then it was over his lap for a terrific blistering. He warmed me up with his hand, then reached for the hairbrush. After the spanking he put me in the corner for fifteen minutes while he fixed himself another drink and talked to me about spanking.

He has always been interested in spanking, as I could have guessed when I visited his apartment and he showed me his collection of paddles, hairbrushes and straps. How did he get interested? His parents had never spanked him, he'd never spanked a girlfriend, even in fun, and he'd never had any unusual experience like seeing a girlfriend spanked.

Suddenly orphaned at sixteen by his parents' death in a car accident, he went to live with a widowed aunt and her two "*very* pretty, *very* scrumptious" daughters, ages thirteen and fifteen. His aunt considered him much more mature and responsible than the girls. To his surprise he was often put in charge of them and with his responsibility came the authority to spank. His aunt was a big fan of old fashioned punishment, the girls were high spirited and often in trouble, and he ended up with one or the other of them over his knee at least once a week.

"And soon enough I became a pro," he told me. "With the hairbrush, the strap and the switch." Always bare bottom. Always with corner time before and after. Always in front of the other girl if she was around.

"They didn't like their spankings," he said. "Not like you," he laughed. "They hated them. They were mortified because they knew they were showing everything and I was barely older than them. In fact, the older one had real feelings for me and the younger one had a puppy crush."

"They practically had anxiety attacks the first few times I spanked them, they were so upset. But they got used to it."

"My aunt also punished the girls by washing their mouths out with soap, when they were lippy or used bad language. (I told you she was old fashioned.) That was usually my job, too. I also could punish them with extra chores, writing lines, or whatever."

"When you're a teenage boy, you haven't lived until you've ordered a girl almost your age to strip, given her a licking with a switch till her cute behind is all stripy, washed her mouth out with soap, then sat her down to write "I will not use bad words" a hundred times before she can rinse out her mouth."

How did the girls feel?

"Interesting. They didn't resent me as much as they might have. I mean, a cousin their age showing up on the doorstep and the next thing they know he's being allowed to strip and spank them? But they got used to it. Once they were over the first shock, they realized I liked them and was actually easier on them than their mother was. When she was going to spank one of them, they'd often ask if I could do it instead. It was so cute."

We both laughed.

"Plus, like I said, they both had a crush on me. So I was happy to do the spankings, the girls were happy to be spanked by me, and my aunt was happy to be relieved of the chore. Win–win all around."

"I guess my feelings about spanking, girls, dominance, submission, and sex all kind of got mixed together," my boyfriend said. "But don't worry, I won't wash *your* mouth out."

That guy admitted he spanks as many women as he can. Sometimes he has sex with them, sometimes their relationship is just spanking. He is not interested in women who won't be spanked. He always takes command in these relationships. He chooses the implement and how hard he uses it. He has his favorite implements: a small over–the–knee paddle called "Daddy's Little Helper" and a longer bend–over–and–assume–the–position paddle he calls "The Board of Education." It's the size of my old sorority paddle but with holes drilled in it. It really stings, take it from me.

I'd like to meet some of the other girls he spanks. It would be a lot of fun to compare notes.

x x x

DOMINATED BY WOMEN WHO SPANK

— BARRY R., PENNSYLVANIA

Maybe those of us who are by nature masochists and submissives carry our need to be spanked from our childhood and, like Peter Pan, never grew up.

I remember very clearly spankings given to me by my mother and a few times by a sister who was ten years older than me. I remember everything — the words, the expressions on their face. My mother, resigned to doing her duty; my sister, acting like it was a burden but eager to punish. I remember that special moment of dread; the mental torment beforehand nearly equaled the physical torment of the spanking itself.

I remember always thinking, "Why did I mess up?" I was always repentant, but it was never possible to avoid a spanking with apologies, and soon my behind would be burning with pain.

It is that strange, bittersweet memory of those moments of dread as the spanking neared, and the pain of the spanking itself, mixed with the closeness of my mother or sister spanking me, that has given me the desire to be controlled and spanked throughout my adult life by the gentler sex.

I would like to share with you and your readers some of my spankings as an adult. My first adult experience was with a woman named Marcie. She was nineteen, dark haired, dark eyed and as pretty as she was aggressive and willful. She liked to use a switch and always had a fresh supply. Her job required a commute along country roads, and she would pull over to cut fresh switches from a suitable tree or bush.

We had just started dating each other. I was relaxing in her living room, and she had gotten annoyed at me for being careless with my drinks and cigarette butts. I told her it was no big deal. She disappeared into her bedroom. A moment later she returned, with a long, threatening–looking apple switch in her hand. She grabbed me by my neck and pushed me to a kneeling position. I was bigger than her and could have resisted but was paralyzed by her anger and the way she took command.

Marcie laid into my bottom and upper thighs with the switch. At the same time she let me know she wouldn't tolerate either slovenly behavior or sass and I'd better listen up when she tried to improve me. She expected me to obey her or I'd get Mr. Switch. She also said she had a nice razor strap if that didn't do the job. I didn't dare try to get away; I stayed on hands and knees while Marcie's switch painted burning lines all over my bottom.

She used the strap as well. The switch gives an awful smart that lingers for a long time, but for sheer pain and punishment and the power to convince, there's nothing like an old fashioned, heavy, supple razor strap wielded by an assertive woman onto a man's bare behind. She used it to punish me for misbehavior like sloppiness around our house (we moved in together), not doing chores, being late, or sass. She also used light strappings and switchings or just teased me about whether she was going to administer them, to get me excited for sex. That worked every time.

After two years of switchings and strappings almost every time we got together, Marcie and I parted. Then her place was taken by another woman who was not only dominant but sadistic. Claudette (beware of women with French names) was twenty–six, red haired, and pretty, but in a hard, trailer–trashy sort of way. She looked like the guards in those awful movies about women in prison. She had a way of looking me up and down that would make me tremble all the way down to my bowels. She intended to be in charge every moment.

Claudette didn't believe in the switch or the strap. She said those were "child's toys." She believed in the *whip*. When we moved in together, she told me she expected obedience and good behavior, or else. She didn't punish me for the first month we were together. But one evening she came home from work upset after a falling out with her boss. Then she found the house a mess. She'd told me to clean the place and I'd forgotten some of the things I was supposed to do. Then I confessed I'd broken her favorite decanter. When I told her that, she looked at me in a way that made my balls shrivel up. I knew I was in for it.

After an angry lecture, Claudette said, "Go to the bedroom and strip down and wait for me in the corner. I'll be in soon enough." She added, "In the meantime, think about your behavior."

After I waited in the corner ten minutes, wondering what would happen, she came in dressed in bra, panties, and high heeled shoes. In her hand she held a coiled, braided, black whip, about three feet long. Just looking at it almost took my breath away. I had never felt a whip before. Never even seen one in person.

She made me lie down on the bed, over a pillow that raised my bottom, and move my legs apart. I was terrified she would hit me on my penis and balls or exposed asshole. But she balled up a towel and put it where it protected my penis and balls. Then she greased a butt plug and pushed it into my anus. It had a wide thick base that protected my anus from any erring whip strokes. The butt plug was large and very uncomfortable but there was no way to get rid of it. "It's designed to stay in," she said. "And you'd better keep it in."

Then she vented her anger on me with that whip, and she was a real expert. If the switch burned, the whip burned ten times worse. All I could do was lie over the pillow, not daring to move, while my poor bottom blazed. Despite my age, I cried like a baby. Such is the power of the whip.

Claudette was inventive in the tasks she assigned me, and the punishments for not performing to her satisfaction. Sometimes she'd strip me and leave me chained to a bolt in the wall, frustrated with discomfort, shame and boredom and worried whether I'd get to use the bathroom before I humiliated myself.

Sometimes she'd make me wear coarse, itchy garments, like burlap diapers, for hours. She washed out my mouth with soap more than once, so I was very careful with my language. She washed *me* out with soapy enemas if washing my mouth out "didn't do the job." Sometimes she'd follow that with screwing me in the ass with a strap–on dildo. "I'll teach you whose job it is to play the man around here," she'd say.

She knew I hated cold showers; sometimes she'd make me stand there while she hosed me down with icy water for minutes.

I have always had the need to be dominated by a strong woman. The woman doesn't have to be physically huge; force of personality is the main thing to ensure dominance. From my personal experience, there are many woman who love nothing more than dominating a man in every way and imposing severe discipline.

My latest girlfriend, Carmen, is 5' 10" — much taller than any previous girlfriend. In fact she has done runway modeling. She's twenty–nine (claims she's younger but I've seen her driver's license), and very quiet and friendly outside the house. But at home, when I do anything to annoy her, it's the strap for yours truly. She has a special strap with three tails on the business end, made in Scotland, called a "tawse."

Carmen punishes me for misdeeds, imagined misdeeds, or just when she's in the mood. If she's had a bad day, I risk getting the strap. Or if it's her time of the month and she gets cramps, it makes her feel better to turn my bottom from white to bright shaking red. One time she came home in a sour mood and I knew I'd better lay low. Still, I got a terrible blistering; she even sponged my bottom down several times during the strapping.

When we were in bed later, she was in a better mood and I asked why she had given me such a fierce strapping.

She ran her hand over my hot behind and said, "I guess I did give you a hard time. But it's good for you."

Then she said, "I had some problems at a shoot. The photographer and I weren't communicating well, he blamed me in front of the client. I had to hold my tongue because its an important client, the makeup girl was an idiot . . . it was one thing after another. Honestly, I was hoping you'd screwed up so I'd have an excuse to punish you."

Then she laughed. "Unfortunately, you hadn't done anything wrong. The place was perfect. But I decided to punish you anyhow."

I didn't say anything, but I thought to myself that what my girlfriends do is what many women would do if they got the chance. They may have been frustrated by a situation where they can't react as they'd like to, but they take it out later on a man. I think many women, probably the great majority, would love to dominate a man, including with severe physical punishment. They may have been trained otherwise, they may not admit it to themselves, but that is their nature, just as it's mine to be dominated by a strong woman.

THE PHILOSOPHY OF THE PADDLE SOLVES JUVENILE DELINQUENCY

— ROB F., BROCKTON, NEW YORK

I assure you the many letters about spanking barely touch this fascinating subject. One important point is that there are really at least two different kinds of spanking: spanking for sexual enjoyment and spanking as a disciplinary measure.

I have strong opinions on spanking as they relate to juvenile delinquency. I would call my approach "The Philosophy of the Paddle."

I believe in child psychology, understanding your child, reasoning with your child and all that, but not at the expense of parental authority. I'm thinking of adolescents, or "teenagers" as they are commonly but loosely called. (Adolescence can start before the teenage years.) These years are a wonderful, exciting time of life, but also a time when the boy or girl needs the most guidance from his or her parents. Suddenly the teenager thinks he knows it all, but really knows just enough, along with a not fully–developed judgment, to get himself in trouble.

There have always been conflicts between teenagers, and their parents, and society at large. If you don't believe me, read *Romeo and Juliette*. What is unusual today, though, is the way adults have let teenagers take control in so many ways. Not only do their degenerate tastes dominate much of fashion, music, ra-

94

dio, TV and movies, but they are a major source of crime.

I doubt anyone has a solution — certainly our present federal government and my city are clueless — but I have a plan worth trying. I firmly believe in corporal punishment of teenagers. Talking to them and reasoning with them have accomplished nothing. Lowering our standards of dress and behavior to appease them has accomplished next to nothing. Isn't it time to reverse course and lay down firm standards of behavior with penalties for violating them? What can we lose by giving it a try?

Some people say that spanking teenagers does no good, even causes resentment and more antisocial behavior. Nonsense! *Any time* someone is punished, there is resentment, but that is so with any punishment, not just corporal punishment. Furthermore, there is greater resentment of *overindulgence*. Either the teenager realizes he needs limits and resents the parents who ignore their duty to impose them; or if his behavior finally gets so bad it cannot be abided, he resents limits that are belatedly imposed.

I think our juvenile courts would accomplish much more if they would appoint men and women who knew how to use a paddle, strap or cane as well as a psychology book in dealing with some of our young miscreants. Perhaps a blistered, throbbing behind would be a greater reminder to behave than a lecI don't know where we got the notion that a teenage boy or girl is too old to be spanked. It certainly wasn't a common view years ago. Far more teenagers were spanked, regularly and severely, years ago. The threat was always there, and not just from their parents. Many a junior high and high school principal had a well–burnished paddle hanging from his office wall or dangling from his belt. Many a police car had a well–used strap or paddle in the trunk. And unlike today, parents would back up these authority figures rather than call up the ACLU to sue them.

Your readers may be asking, "What does he know about the subject?" My background consists of a college degree in statistics with a minor in child psychology. I work as an insurance actuary. I am married and we have two children, a boy of 17 and a girl of 16. My wife and I discussed child raising before we were married, and both believe firmly in spanking for discipline. Both our children are still spanked, even at their advanced ages. Our daughter is spanked only by my wife; when she reached 12 my wife and I decided that she was too old to be spanked by me, especially since she was starting to develop and we always spanked bare bottom. However, I do witness her spankings to show that my wife and I back each other up when discipline is necessary.

My son went through a disobedient stage for awhile but has been spanked only four or five times in the last three years. The only recent time was a few months ago when he and his friends had too much beer one night. Around midnight they decided to "t.p." the house of a girl who had snubbed one of them. "T.P." means throwing strings of toilet paper all over the branches of the trees in front of the house. The girl and her family weren't around, but as luck would have it a neighbor spotted them and came out. He didn't identify them and they had thoughtfully covered the cars' license plates with mud so he couldn't get those either. However, in their rush to escape, the two getaway cars scraped each other, and one of those was our car, driven by our son.

After discussing the matter with my wife, I yanked my son's license for four weeks and also sentenced him to two sessions with the paddle. I took him into the garage and whacked away at his bare backside as hard as I'd ever given it to him. By the end his backside was the color of raw hamburger and hot to the touch. He was shaking like a leaf and crying the same as when he was much younger.

After the paddling, I hugged him, told him how much it hurt his mother and me to learn he was making bad decisions and endangering himself, and reminded him of our absolute, unconditional love. However, he still got the second installment of his paddling punishment two weeks later to reinforce the lesson.

Our daughter, who is presently going through a difficult spell, gets punished far more often. Sometimes it seems like she's dropping her panties and bending over almost every week. She gets punished the same as our son, since my wife and I believe our children should be treated the same and girls shouldn't be coddled more than boys. Besides, her female bottom is more padded than her muscular brother's, so there's no reason she can't take a similar paddling despite her age.

Our daughter's most recent punishment was just a week ago. She failed to come home by our very reasonable curfew, which is also the town's curfew for minors. Then it turned out she and her girlfriends had been smoking and drinking. (Never mind how we found out; daddies have ways.) When confronted, she falsely denied the facts.

The curfew violation, along with the smoking and drinking, called for punishment. The lying called for extra punishment. As I said, my wife administers punishment to our daughter, but I was present for moral support and to quell any resistance.

Our daughter's punishment took place in the den just before her bedtime. She reported in thin cotton pajamas as ordered by my wife. My wife's idea is that these reduce her from a young lady testing her limits to a child submitting to her parent's authority and control. The pajamas wouldn't provide much protection, but our daughter still had to drop them and bend over the back of a low sofa with her arms stretched out and her legs apart, a position that tightens all the slack out of her buttocks. Then my wife gave her a hearty paddling. She used the same paddle I use with my son, similar to the ones used in the few schools that still paddle students. It's oak, with a long handle and holes drilled in the business part.

Our daughter isn't as tough as our son and started crying when she was put in position, even before the first stroke landed. The crying is as much from the humiliation of that position that opens her up so much as from the anticipated pain of the paddling. But she cried a lot louder when my wife gave her thirteen mighty swats.

I felt for my daughter in her pain. She has a beautiful body, especially her buttocks and legs, and it was painful for me to see it punished and turning cherry red. But she knew our rules, she had screwed up royally and the punishment was for her own good. She bawled like a child and wept all over the sofa cushions, but still managed to stay in position the whole way. I was so proud of my brave little trooper.

Our daughter, too, gets hugs and reassurance from her parents after a paddling, and she says this means a lot to her. She just clung to me afterward. She says it's "horribly embarrassing to show everything, but it's comforting at the same time to know you care."

My wife and I don't believe in frequent paddlings. If they are too frequent they are probably not doing much good. It is better to have much more severe and less frequent paddlings. Corporal punishment must be real punishment, never a joke. We believe it should be the final punishment, for serious misbehavior or when other punishment doesn't do the trick, not the first resort. The threat should be sufficiently dire that the offender will change his or her behavior to avoid a spanking.

Although I mentioned my daughter's feeling of humiliation at her exposure, the pain of the spanking itself should be the real deterrent, not the embarrassment, although the latter does make the punishment worse, especially with girls at our daughter's age. At the very least, the offender should have trouble sitting after the punishment and for some hours afterward.

Many people wonder how to spank a teenager, since they are often big enough to put up a fight. It isn't that difficult, especially with girls. Many teenagers will submit without resistance to their parent's authority, especially if their parents have been reasonable and they know they are in the wrong.

But even if an upset and energetic teenager may not be willing to submit to having his bare buttocks punished, certain measures will deal with any reluctance. If outside help is needed, a spouse, relative, neighbor or pastor will assist. Most teenagers would rather submit quietly to a spanking than be spanked anyhow with the help of another person, and get a worse spanking as well as an audience on account of their resistance.

Our daughter has always submitted without resistance. However, one time when I was not home to help my wife, she refused to be paddled. My wife called in the girl's first cousin; he was willing when he found out what she had done.

He is only two years older than our daughter and she had a huge schoolgirl crush on him. Her cousin held her in place, bare buttocks and all, while my wife paddled her, with extras for putting up such a fuss. Then she had to stand in the corner, clothes at her ankles and flaming buttocks on display, while my wife and our nephew visited. It's a very traumatic experience for a thirteen–year–old girl to be punished bare bottom with the assistance of a boy she idolizes.

After that incident, if our daughter hesitated for even a second, my wife would only have to say, "Do you want me to call up Brad to help out?" and our daughter would rush to obey.

If the corporal punishment is handled correctly, it should be rare to need outside help. Explain that if you have to get someone else to assist, the spanking will be harder or more strokes, and the child will have the embarrassment of a witness. Once that is made clear, or carried out as in the case of our daughter, the problem goes away.

In some cases it is best to tie the child's hands. I realize this sounds horrible but it is for the spanked child's own good and also will speed things up. Is it worse to secure the child's hands in order to administer a punishment that will do a world of good, or to fail to administer the punishment with the result that they end up a client of the justice system? Tying down the hands doesn't mean you're going to be brutal with your child; it merely secures them for a spanking of appropriate severity.

Many instruments can be used, and commonsense is the by-word. I repeat that the idea is pain and perhaps humiliation, not beating or injury. I have always been partial to the paddle, but it shouldn't be too narrow, too heavy or too long. Fraternity and sorority paddles are widely available, but I think many of these are too heavy and long, packing too much of a wallop. I prefer something slightly wider and lighter; you don't want to inflict injury; just pain.

I do not claim to be an expert on other implements of corporal punishment. However, razor straps, belts, tawses (Scottish tailed straps), switches (many trees are suitable; birch and hickory are the best known) and canes (more popular in England than here) are commonly used. For over–the–knee spankings, hairbrushes, short–handled bath brushes, and ping pong paddles are ideal. The hand can be used but may leave the spanker stinging as much as the spanked youngster.

The old fashioned baring of buttocks should also be carefully thought out by parents, especially if they are spanking a teenage girl. Spankings are more effective on the bare bottom. They are also more humiliating, especially so in the case of a daughter being spanked by her father.

The reasons to spank bare are safety (better aim, judge the damage), tradition and humiliation as part of the punishment. The arguments against spanking bare are that the girl is already humiliated enough being spanked. She doesn't need the further humiliation of exposing her sexual parts or (in the case of over–the–knee punishment) even having them in contact with her parents' legs, and that it is simply "inappropriate."

In any case, whether the parents spank their teenagers on bare buttocks or allow them underwear (any more clothing is ridiculous), the spanking should be reasonable, not cruel. With the paddle we use, the eight to thirteen hard whacks on the bare buttocks I administer is extremely painful, not just during the spanking but for hours afterward. My wife, being weaker, gives several more. In extreme cases, I have given as much as fifteen. If the offense is beyond all bounds, I don't give more, but schedule a second paddling a week or two later. That gives the errant child something unpleasant to look forward to, and anticipation is almost as painful as the event itself.

If it's an over–the–knee punishment, I wouldn't set a number in advance. Instead, I judge when the spanking is sufficient by the color and heat of the buttocks, the child's crying and trembling, and whether the child's loud cries of remorse and promises not to repeat the bad behavior seem heartfelt. I believe every parent can judge these things.

Perhaps bringing the paddle out of the closet, along with its brethren the strap, cane, hairbrush, et. al., will help restore sanity and parental control to the adult–teenager relationship, and much better behavior in public places.

I enjoy the spanking letters very much and look forward to others' response to my Philosophy of the Paddle.

x x x

OVER HER BOSS'S KNEE

— FRANCIE C., NEW YORK, NEW YORK

I am 18, single, and work as a receptionist and clerk to a very nice gentleman who runs a small sales rep business. Our tiny office is in a prestigious building on Park Avenue in New York City just to gloss our image. In fact, my boss and the other employees travel constantly and mostly work out of their homes and cars. My job is to answer the phone and get rid of nuisances my boss doesn't want to see, just as drop in salesmen and job applicants and the occasional religious fanatic. While answering the phone as needed, I do simple filing and other clerical tasks. It's a surprisingly well paid job, and best of all an easy bus ride from my apartment.

One day my boss asked me to pull the files for an important customer and pack them in a briefcase for him to pick up before he drove to a meeting with them. Unfortunately I pulled the wrong files (the client was *Smythe* Company; I pulled the *Smith* Company files). Fortunately, on the way to the meeting my boss stopped at a diner to review the files over coffee, and caught my mistake. I had to grab a taxi to bring him the correct files. He was able to push the meeting back an hour but it was awkward and embarrassing and also disrupted the rest of his day's schedule.

My boss was furious, but all he said was, "This is unacceptable. We're going to have a talk about this when I get back." Since he wasn't due back until the next afternoon, that gave me almost two days to get worried. But I was certainly careful about my work in the meantime.

The next day he called at 4:45 p.m. and asked me to stay after closing time (5:00 p.m.) for our discussion. At 5:00 p.m. he walked in, went straight through to his office and fifteen minutes later called me in.

"Do you realize what your blunder could have cost me?" he asked. "A major account."

"You can't sleepwalk through your day," he said.

"Am I making unreasonable demands?" he asked.

"No, sir," I said.

"Am I paying you fairly?"

"Yes, sir," He was paying me generously.

"You're doing a good job in some ways," he said.

I felt better.

"But in other ways, you persist in messing up. If yesterday had been an airplane, you would have crashed it." My boss was a private pilot and liked to compare good work and bad work to flying an airplane.

"If you were my daughter, I'd say what you need is a good spanking to get you to change your work attitude. Unfortunately, you aren't, so I'm going to have to let you go."

Under other circumstances I don't know what I would have said. But it was a great job, I would have trouble getting another in the depressed economy at that time, and I knew I'd messed up badly and wanted to make things right.

So I said, "If you think it will help, please go ahead and give me a spanking. I know I deserve it."

That took him aback. He said, "I'd love to spank you, and it *would* do you good, but you know how it is these days — you'd sue me for everything I was worth."

That upset me because I was sincere. It was a genuine offer. Did he think I was setting him up? I explained that I was being honest. I even wrote out a note for him:

"I have made a series of careless mistakes, including pulling the Smith files instead of the Smythe files, which might have cost the company a major account. I have therefore given Mr. Holloway

full authority to spank me as punishment for my errors and in the hope of improving my work, and place myself under his authority."

There was some more, but that was the gist. I signed and dated the note, and even inked my thumb with a stamp pad to put a thumb print next to my signature and make it official.

Mr. Holloway looked at me carefully, rubbed his chin and said, "Please lock the outside door and join me in my office."

I did so. I'm not sure what I was expecting, but his next words were, "Please bring me your hairbrush." I did as told. Then he made me lie across his desk holding onto the far side, and gave me a dozen good hard whacks on each bottom mound. That's what he told me; it *felt* like a lot more.

Despite my age, I cried. It hurt an awful lot. It was like fire all over my behind. I knew I could have gotten up at any time; he wouldn't have forced me back down. But I didn't do so. I wanted to be spanked hard to atone for my errors and I didn't want to disappoint him by breaking my word. I would have clung to the desk even if he had given me a hundred smacks with that horrid hairbrush.

When he finished, he asked, "Do you think I've spanked you enough, or do you need more?"

"Enough, sir. Please, no more," I said through my tears.

Mr. Holloway said he'd keep my note and show it to me whenever I made a mistake, to encourage better work. He also said he wasn't going to fire me, but I should "consider myself on probation."

About a month later, I ushered a man into Mr. Holloway's office that I knew he didn't want to deal with. When my boss had gotten rid of him, he called me in and I took my hairbrush and presented it to him.

He said, "Either you showed him in out of sheer forgetfulness or you showed him in on purpose. Either way, you have earned a spanking."

So, after work, for the second time I reported for a spanking. My boss said that this time he wasn't so angry, it was just an annoyance, not a risk of real damage to the company, but I had either messed up again or deliberately misbehaved.

So, he concluded, "I'm going to deal with it."

This time he had me pull over a straight backed, armless chair. He sat down, saying, "Get over my knee." I didn't do it right at first, so he adjusted me, to my embarrassment. "Lift up, scoot forward," etc. I ended up well over his lap, with my behind up in the air and my hands supporting me on the floor.

It's surprising what one remembers. I remember anticipating the spanking with a strange mixture of excitement and dread, while staring at the pattern of the hardwood floor inches from my face. I remember there were a few paper clips that had fallen there.

He turned up my dress and his hand went to my panties. I objected that it wasn't right, he wasn't my father. But he ordered me to raise up an inch, and I obeyed. He worked my panties down. I blushed but stayed where I belonged.

"You are getting your bottom spanked this time, not your clothing," he said. "Evidently the other lesson didn't take. So this will be a little firmer, and if this lesson doesn't take, the next will be firmer, until we get the point across."

Then my boss rained spanks on my bare bottom, very hard, with little pause between spanks. Sometimes he would switch from side to side, other times he landed several one after another on the same spot, so I never knew what to expect and couldn't prepare for the pain of even one spank. The spanks rang out in that small room. They stung so much! I felt like my bottom was on a griddle. He found every tender spot I had. I wriggled and squirmed and he had to put me back in position several times before starting in again.

Still, I knew I was getting a well deserved punishment and that it was good for me. He finally stopped, still holding me over his lap, and asked whether I had learned my lesson. I asked him to spank me until I couldn't cry any more. He said he'd be happy to and it would do me good. Then he reached for the hairbrush.

The hairbrush was much more painful than his hand, especially smacking on my already burning flesh. It made its own loud sound with each spank, and somehow he managed to find new tender spots. I felt like I was being branded and blistered. I cried until I couldn't cry any more, just lay over his lap breathing roughly with my behind shaking with each hairbrush spank. I knew the punishment was fair, and it was an emotional release as well.

Those two spankings set the pattern. Usually my work was excellent; the spankings were a good influence on me! But sometimes I'd mess up and get spanked. And sometimes I'd mess up deliberately and get spanked much worse, with Mr. Holloway's hard hand, then my hairbrush. In fact I wrote Mr. Holloway another note:

PERMISSION TO SPANK

In the hope of improving my attitude and work, I hereby give Mr. Holloway full authority to punish me by spanking, whenever he deems it necessary, and in whatever manner, with whatever instrument, and with whatever severity he deems appropriate, and upon bare buttocks as he deems appropriate, and I will obediently submit to such spankings and his authority to administer same, for the remainder of my employment here.

(Signed, dated, thumbprint)

For my birthday, Mr. Holloway gave me a gift of two beautiful hairbrushes, one of which stayed in his desk. We both feel the spankings are good for my work and attitude. They must have done me good; painful as they are, I enjoy them now!

x x x

ROOMMATES MAINTAIN HARMONY WITH A RAZOR STRAP

— JANICE R., PASADENA, CALIFORNIA

I'm a working woman sharing a large apartment with three friends. We are all between 21 and 24. We have an arrangement among ourselves, and I wonder how many other young women in similar circumstances also have such an arrangement.

When girls live at home the parents act as authority to maintain good behavior around the house (and outside it). Sometimes the older children have some authority over the younger ones, especially in the parents' absence, but the parents' word is final and they are to be respected. However, when the girls grow up, leave home and (typically) share a house or apartment, there can be problems.

The young women may feel since they are on their own, without parents to order them around, they may do whatever they wish. They can be inconsiderate of others' feelings, including their housemates'. That happened in my case where there was constant friction among the four of us. We had clear house rules but didn't have a way of enforcing the rules to keep harmony in our apartment.

Things came to a head when we all planned a large party for a friend who was getting married. Each of us was given tasks to do. One of the girls, Anne, had the day off from work, so she was given the job of cleaning. (We would make it up to her by doing more chores later.) However, when the rest of us got home we found the place a pigpen. It turned out that Anne slept late and then went out on a movie matinee date, completely forgetting about her cleaning. The rest of us had to do her work as well as our own.

We were all pretty mad, and one of us said, "What Anne needs is a good spanking, and I would be happy to do it if you need a volunteer." But Anne, when she finally returned, said she wasn't the only one to have forgotten her work; all of us had messed up plenty of times. (True.)

After dinner we discussed how to maintain order for the tenth time, and finally came to the conclusion that we *all* required discipline. There was no practical way to "ground" each other or take away privileges, which would require supervision among other problems. Lecturing and scolding each other would be absurd, since we were all the same age and wouldn't listen to lectures anyhow.

Finally, we decided the only thing that might make sense and be effective was . . . spanking. None of us *liked* the idea, but none of us had any *better* solution. This was all we could think of after many tries. So, although with a lot of nervousness, we all agreed.

We set up rules, with one night a week chosen for hearings. If one girl said she was wronged by another, she could calendar the matter. If a girl had done something that affected everyone, anyone could calendar the matter.

On hearing night, each case would be brought up in turn. If it was one against one, the accuser and accused would each present her side to the other two for decision. If there was a violation of a house rule, thus affecting everyone, the accused would give her side and the other three would decide on guilt. The accused could also admit her fault and ask for leniency.

If the offending girl was to be spanked, she would be blindfolded and sent to wait standing in the corner. Then the other girls would pick cards to decide who would give the punishment. That way the punished girl wouldn't know who was spanking her and couldn't bear a grudge.

We all agreed that if any good was to come of our new arrangement, the spanking would have to be serious and hard. We bought a barber's razor strap for the purpose. The girl's hands were to be tied so she was helpless and could not take off the blindfold.

The fear of that formidable razor strap kept all of us well behaved for weeks, e, but soon we started falling off the wagon. Mary got written up for leaving a mess in the bathroom, and the two judges agreed that the culprit must be spanked. She at first resisted, but the other three pointed out we had all agreed and she had to keep her word.

The culprit was blindfolded, had her hands tied and was put in the corner to await her fate. The chastiser was chosen by picking cards, and we all gently guided Mary to the couch, where we bent her over. All three of us had the task of baring Mary's bottom and thighs.

The moment we started taking down her clothes, she began crying and begging us not to carry out the punishment. She said she would accept any other punishment if only we wouldn't strap her. However, there was no turning back. We had to carry out the punishment, not only for her good but as an example for the rest of us. So down came her skirt, and down came her panties to reveal her buttocks. One of us asked her whether she could stay in position or we needed to hold her there. "I'll stay," she sobbed.

The girl who administered the strap was either born with the skill, or had experience, or had found time to practice for this day. She really laid it on, judging by the way the culprit screamed with each stroke, cried and trembled. It was obvious the well chosen judicial instrument was imposing plenty of pain, judging from her bawling and carrying on. But Mary didn't try to get up. She didn't want the added indignity of having to be held down, and she knew misbehaving would mean added punishment. It was remarkable to see her poor buttocks color up, first with a light pink blush, then a deeper pink, finally reaching a rich red hue. Hot to the touch, too; we all felt them.

Soon enough, though, the punishment was over, with Mary

helplessly draped crying over the couch. We put the strap away (for Mary to clean and oil later to reinforce her lesson). Then her hands were untied, the blindfold was removed, and she was left in the corner, cherry buttocks still bare, to cry for ten minutes and think about her behavior and punishment.

The next morning in the bathroom we could see Mary's buttocks were covered with red streaks, and she had trouble sitting at breakfast. I wondered how she was going to get through eight hours at her work desk. But the punishment seemed to have made an impression. She was apologetic to the girl she had upset and told all of us we had certainly found a method of discipline "that would make any of us think three times before breaking the rules or being inconsiderate." She didn't hold her punishment against any of us, even whichever one had administered the strap.

That was the first of about a dozen punishments so far. The apartment is always neat and clean, we get along much better, and we have a warm relationship with each other. It is odd how punishing the bare buttocks of a housemate makes me feel closer to that girl, and how being bent over, bared and getting the strap myself makes me feel closer to my roommates, almost as if they were standing in for my parents for those painful minutes.

All of us now realize that even though we are living independently, we still have obligations to each other and must be considerate. We have all felt the strap and we all feel it is just the instrument to help our behavior. We all agree that every time a girl has been strapped she has deserved it; we have never had any disagreement about whether a punishment was deserved and only some small ones about how severe it should be.

None of us likes being punished this way. We don't understand other women who write that they get wildly excited sexually from being punished this way. For us, a punishment with the strap means nothing but pain and more pain, along with the humiliation of the corner time afterward. No pleasure at all.

We give each other from eight to sixteen licks with the strap. Mary, just like the first time, starts crying when she is stripped, before the first swat even lands. The rest of us try to be brave but are always crying after the first three or four from strap. The pain is shocking!

Painful as these punishments are, we all feel they do us a world of good and plan to continue our arrangement. One of us, Anita, is leaving in four months and when we look for a replacement housemate we will explain our system and make sure she is willing to abide by it.

x x x

SPANKED BY HIS TEACHER

— RANDY D., PORTSMOUTH, NEW HAMPSHIRE

A m I a masochist or spanking fetishist? I don't know, but I do know I get great pleasure from being spanked.

I don't know how my interest started. I got my first spanking at age 13. My parents had divorced when I was small, then my mother died and I ended up living with a widowed aunt. She was strict, but didn't spank me; when I misbehaved she gave me chores.

The spanking came from a teacher named Miss Proctor. She was only in her late twenties and so pretty all the boys had a crush on her. But she was very strict, a real disciplinarian. I was a rowdy boy, got into plenty of mischief and was in her bad books more than once.

One evening, my aunt and I had to go to the school to talk with Miss Proctor. After the three of us discussed my behavior, my aunt and my teacher discussed it with each other, with me at the other end of the classroom. I couldn't hear much, but I knew that various punishments were discussed. I didn't like their expressions, and the way they kept glancing at me made me nervous. When we went home, my aunt said that I would be visiting Miss Proctor after school the next day.

Sure enough, I had to stay after school the next day and walked to Miss Proctor's house with her. I remember it was a beautiful crisp Fall day, with red, yellow and orange color in every leaf. I was nervous about what was going to happen, but still it felt special to be alone with her. Some of my friends saw us walking. I wondered what they thought.

When we got to Miss Proctor's house, she said, "You have been a problem for months. I have discussed the matter with your aunt, and she has given me her blessing to punish you. You are going to get a spanking. If you give me any trouble, I will summon the gentleman next door to assist me, and you will get a much worse spanking. Do we understand each other?"

We understood each other, all right.

"Go to that bedroom and remove all your clothes. Every stitch. You may keep your socks on if you wish. Then sit on the stool. I will be back in five minutes and you had best be nude as the day you were born."

Beautiful as she was, she was all business. I did as ordered. I was very nervous as I stripped. I was physically shy. I hated even stripping for my doctor, and here I was stripping to be punished. I sat naked on the hard stool — it was more like ten minutes — and didn't dare move, and it got uncomfortable after a while.

Miss Proctor finally came in, and she was carrying a long strap. She made me lie on the bed over a big pillow, with my legs spread. At thirteen I was very aware of my suddenly developing body, and I felt mortified displaying myself where I knew she could see everything. Even my doctor never looked at my butthole when I saw him once a year.

Then that beautiful, stern lady whipped me with her strap on my bare behind until it was bright red and burned like there were hot coals on it. She whipped me again and again with that horrible strap. I tried not to cry in front of her, then I decided I'd better cry so she might feel sorry for me. I don't think it made a difference; she had decided how many I was going to get, and it didn't matter if I bawled like a baby or toughed it out.

After the spanking was over, Miss Proctor made me stand in front of her, facing away. She squeezed my butt and I almost jumped from the pain.

"Good," she said, "I have your attention. Something I've never managed in class."

Then she made me turn around and I was mortified all over again, with her looking at my thirteen–year–old penis and balls.

Miss Proctor told me I would be coming to her house once a week for a similar spanking until my conduct improved. Then the spankings would stop but they'd start again if I misbehaved. All with my aunt's approval. Then she finally let me get dressed.

"By the way, you're a very good looking boy," she said. "And big for your age." I was still so shaken up by the spanking that I didn't figure out till later what *that* meant.

When I got home, my aunt made me lower my pants and underwear, inspected my butt with approval and told me she was planning to give me a spanking herself but I looked too sore for that. I was so grateful I thanked her again and again. But she said I shouldn't be thanking her; she was just putting it off a day or two so my bottom could recover.

During class the next day it was misery to sit. Miss Proctor saw and smiled at me out of the corner of her mouth. I prayed that no one else would figure out what happened. Some kids asked me why I was with her after school but I said I was helping her paint her kitchen.

After school two days later, my aunt made me pull down my pants and underwear and inspected me. I had to get over her lap, and she gave me a thrashing with a large, heavy, old fashioned ebony wood hairbrush on my still pink bottom, and once again I had trouble sitting in class the following day.

After this, my behavior improved, but it lapsed at times. Then my aunt would spank me, always bare bottom over her lap with that hairbrush. When my misbehavior happened at school, Miss Proctor would take me home with her for the strap.

She was a real ace at spanking me and I never knew exactly what to expect. But one thing was predictable; I'd have to take off all my clothes first. Besides the strap, she was skillful with the switch, a there were several handy trees in her back yard. She also would put me over her lap and whack me with her hairbrushes; a rectangular oak one and an oval walnut one.

Painful as these punishments from Miss Proctor were, I came to enjoy them. I didn't enjoy one minute of my aunt's spankings, but these were different — Miss Proctor was so young, pretty, firm, wore the nicest perfume — I had a crush and no doubt about it. I would misbehave at school to receive my teacher's punishments.

One time, as Miss Proctor got started spanking me, her doorbell rang. She told me to go lie on her bed and close the door. The visitor was a spinster friend of hers. Miss Proctor told her she'd been in the middle of disciplining an errant student, and let the other woman watch my punishment. I was embarrassed but the embarrassment somehow added a kick of extra excitement.

I want to emphasize that Miss Proctor *saw* everything I had but never *touched* anything she shouldn't have. I know this happens in some cases. The closest she came was one time when after the spanking she said I looked flushed and I admitted I felt feverish. She made me lie down on my stomach and took my temperature, *rectally*, with her hand on my butt holding in the thermometer. I was *totally* embarrassed but felt very safe and cared for. She said I did have a fever and should have told her so she could have put off my spanking until I felt better.

My spankings from my aunt kept on right through my teens; once she'd started, she decided they did me good. Sadly, Miss Proctor only spanked me for five months. After that she moved to a better job in a distant city.

I am now 24, single, and have my own apartment near the town where I went to school. I still enjoy getting spanked. Although I have an active sex life, to my surprise I have had trouble finding women my own age who are happy to spank me. Fortunately, there is a neighbor down the hall who believes in spanking young men and women of any age.

"Mrs. Doe" is a divorcee in her early thirties, halfway between the ages of my aunt and Miss Proctor back when they started disciplining me. She is the assistant headmistress at a private girls' boarding school and known for her firmness there. With me, she demands neatness, cleanliness, regular habits, and good attitudes and behavior. Every Thursday evening she does a white glove inspection of my apartment and quizzes me about my behavior during the week. If my sheets aren't changed, or my bed is unmade, or the kitchen messy, or I've forgotten to take out the garbage, or I've even left the toothpaste cap off or the toothbrush on the counter rather than in its holder, my punishment is a spanking on my bare bottom. Ditto if I've slacked at work, procrastinated about anything, dressed sloppy, or otherwise had less than perfect behavior.

The procedure is almost always the same. Mrs. Doe discusses my behavior or faults with me. Not really a discussion; she sits and goes over the problems, while I stand at attention in front of her and answer "yes, ma'am," "no, ma'am" and "I apologize, ma'am."

Then she tells me, "Prepare yourself for a sound spanking, young man." This means I must strip in front of her and put my clothes away neatly in my closet. The first time she punished me I made the mistake of tossing them on my bed, and I haven't made that mistake again! Then I go to the living room where I bend over the arm of my sofa with my hands on the sofa and my legs slightly apart. This of course tightens my buttocks and puts them in a good spanking position, and also exposes my penis and balls, which I still find embarrassing but exciting.

Then Mrs. Doe pulls out her spanking implement. Occasionally it's a cane, but usually it's a strap, very much like the one Miss Proctor introduced me to, except that Mrs. Doe's strap is black while Miss Proctor's was dark brown, and Mrs. Doe's is cut into three tails for the last foot.

Mrs. Doe straps me until I cry and promise to improve my behavior and not to repeat the fault. However, as much as I cry or promise, it never shortens the punishment or makes her lighten her swats. My behavior must be perfect during the spanking. If she thinks I'm not taking my "correction" well, I am treated to additional swats. I am always left with a burning, throbbing, swollen bottom that is painful to sit on. The color doesn't leave for more than a day.

Mrs. Doe is a real professional with her strap. In her position at the school, she has the task of spanking the students. Since she administers at least two or three punishments a week, and has been the assistant four years, she's had hundreds of chances to build up good form and strong muscles. At the school, though, girls are allowed to keep panties on during their spanking. "More's the pity," says Mrs. Doe.

One time she spanked me so hard, really more on the upper thigh than buttock, that I yelled "Jesus Christ!" That wasn't a good idea. When she got through with the strap, she took me in the bathroom where she washed my mouth out with soap (an awful punishment I'd never suffered from my aunt or Miss Proctor although my language was often bad as a teenager). With the horrible taste of the soap still filling my mouth, she bent me over the bathtub side and gave me a soapy *enema*. She filled the hand syringe again and again, lubricating me deeply with soap on her finger before each insertion.

"That should help clean out your bad language," she said. Since then I've managed to hold my tongue while she spanked me.

Mrs. Doe always wears business clothes, the same as she wears at her school, while spanking me. I always feel like a little boy being punished by a beautiful yet strict schoolteacher, just as I felt with Miss Proctor. Just as I felt with Miss Proctor, I wouldn't mind going much farther with Mrs. Doe, but she has never touched me except to tuck my balls and penis safely out of the way before a spanking, and the time she gave me the enema.

Mrs. Doe's notion is that spanking does everyone good whatever their age, and especially young men and women. She believes a spanking should include both pain and humiliation. That's why I have to undress in front of her and must be completely nude. To increase the humiliation, she sometimes invites one of her woman friends to watch me be lectured, stripped and spanked, and that loss of privacy is even more humiliating.

However, I have to admit I not only get a thrill out of the spankings, but they improve my behavior and tidiness. Still, every spanking is agony, breathtakingly painful.

Mrs. Doe and I have had our arrangement for two years. I am now "engaged to be engaged" to a beautiful and strong willed girlfriend. We have a great sex life together. She has mentioned that she was spanked as a small girl, and when she was sixteen, she was often in charge of her younger brother (13) and sister

(12) and spanked them with her mother's approval. She described the punishments as "real spankings," pants or panties down, over the knee with her hand and hairbrush "till they were the color of Santa Claus's coat."

My girlfriend didn't tell me she got a sexual thrill out of spanking her brother and sister, but she said she enjoyed the authority and it improved their behavior. Neither of us has mentioned the idea of her spanking me, but I'm going to broach the subject next week if she doesn't do so first.

x x x

THE PAINFUL HAIRBRUSH

— GABRIELLA G., SHREVEPORT, LOUISIANA

As a child I was never spanked by my parents, and as a teen only rarely. I overheard my parents discussing the subject one time. My mother was for spanking me. "It will do her good," etc. ("No, mom, it won't!" I thought.) But my father was against it. "She's fourteen, honey. She's got hair and boobs. It really isn't decent." (Go, Daddy! Darn right I have boobs! Great ones!)

The result was a compromise of sorts. First off, my mother did all the spankings. Daddy didn't have to.

Second, I wasn't spanked often; only for really wild behavior.

Third, there was no humiliation. I mean being stripped completely, having to request a spanking, standing in the corner, having my brother (23 and living at home while he went to grad school) watch my punishment — nothing like that.

But fourth, when I *was* spanked, it was a real shellacking. Over mom's knee, panties down, with a hairbrush, until my behind was beet red and hot and I cried so hard my breath got ragged.

Still, spankings were few and far between. Mom wasn't mean. She didn't get a charge out of spanking me. She just thought a spanking was effective when I got too far out of line, which wasn't very often. I only got spanked about once every three or four months, and when I reached 16 the spankings ended.

But when I was 17, when my parents had marriage problems and were temporarily separated, I had to go live with my uncle (my mom's brother) and aunt and their family. Then my mom got sick and my dad wasn't able to take care of me because he was at a military post overseas. It was kind of complicated.

My uncle and aunt made me feel at home, and so did their two sons. One was fifteen, the other a few months older than me, and we got along great. They both enjoyed having a girl in the house, and the younger one had a crush on me.

But within days of my arrival, I was shocked to find out my two boy cousins were often spanked. I learned this when I came home from school, walked into the living room and found my younger cousin over his mom's lap, with her whaling away on his very cute behind with a small paddle, while he cried and pleaded.

I was fascinated. My cousin begged his mom to send me away, but she ordered me to stay and watch the rest of his spanking, adding embarrassment to pain as an additional punishment. I was embarrassed too, but was happy I could stay and watch without being blamed for taking advantage. After all, I was just obeying my aunt.

My aunt had her own method of spanking. She'd give three or four right after the other on one spot and my poor cousin's legs would spasm and flip upward from the pain. Then she'd look around, find another good spot, and give him three or four there. She had his closer leg pinned under her right leg, so there was no way he could escape. That also opened his legs up completely and I could see his balls and winking button and a bit of his dick from where I stood behind him.

I liked my cousin but still enjoyed his punishment and embarrassment and seeing his parts. After his spanking he had to stand in the corner with his bare bottom, now bright red, still showing and his arms at his side, no rubbing allowed.

A few days later I messed up and learned I was an equal member of the household. I couldn't believe it when I was ordered to strip in front of both my cousins. I could feel the heat of my face flushing. But soon my bottom was hot and redder than my face, as my aunt punished me with her paddle.

My aunt did me the same way I had seen my cousin punished. With her pinning down one leg to hold me in place and separate my legs, I knew I was showing my cousins everything I had. But during the spanking I wasn't thinking of the show I was giving them, but only of the pain. It hurt like the devil. I yelled and cried and promised to be good, but it still went on a long time.

I had a lot of pain afterward and felt very embarrassed standing in the corner. ("No shuffling around, no touching your butt, hands at sides.") Even though I was embarrassed, I also was excited in a weird way. Once I was out of the corner and had my clothes back on, I decided that despite the pain, I still liked it, just as I liked seeing my cousins get punished. After that I never *asked* for a spanking, but managed to get in trouble every few weeks, knowing my bottom would pay the price.

Despite my cousins' embarrassment at being spanked in front of me, the family was casual about nudity. Dad and mom always had clothes on, but the boys often went around nude in the house and backyard and they even took me to a nudist resort once. I went row boating without sunblock and got sunburned where it hurt most, but that's another story. It's interesting that it wasn't at all erotic to see my cousins in the nude, once I got used to the novelty, but it was *very* erotic to see them getting spanked, or have them seeing me getting spanked. I liked them both, especially the younger one, but we never shared more than a brotherly–sisterly kiss or hug.

I was disappointed when I went back to live with my mom and the spankings ended. I wanted to be spanked so much I very carefully approached three girlfriends. So carefully I'm not sure they even understood they were being propositioned to spank me. I just happened to mention the spankings in my uncle and aunt's house and watched their reactions. Their reactions were, #1: "Yuk!"; #2: "I can't believe it! I'd have just died"; and #3: "That's child abuse!" Anyhow, they obviously weren't interested in either spanking me or getting spanked, which I also wanted to try.

I was afraid to approach boyfriends. It was a small town.

I didn't get spanked again until I was in college and became a glutton for punishment. I also got into bondage, "candle play" (having hot wax dripped on me), and age play (treating a boy-friend like a baby). But that's another story.

LAURIE'S CHOICE OF PUNISHMENTS

— DAN V., BAD AXE, MICHIGAN

Spanking should not be a subject only for sex surveys and studies. I think few people use spanking for either the spanker or spankee to get sexually excited. Most spankings are given for discipline. They give little pleasure to the spanker, who is often resorting to spanking only when other discipline has failed; and they give even less pleasure to the spankee.

My own daughter Laurie has had many a sound bottom warming in her 17 years, but she shows no sign of developing a liking for being spanked. She has a dozen arguments why we shouldn't redden her tail; if she enjoyed it I don't think she'd protest so much. And if she enjoyed it she would give us more reasons to spank her than she does. On the contrary, she behaves very well, better than most of her friends, and can go for a month without an over–the–knee appointment.

Nor do I enjoy spanking my daughter. I look for reasons to let her off with a warning or talking to. In a way it does "hurt me more than it hurts her," and my wife often has to insist that our darling be given the paddle. And that she be bared for it. And that I keep paddling her, long after I'm ready to end the spanking and put her in the corner to cry, display her reddened rear and try to rub away the pain.

As you can see, my wife and I disagree with those who say teenaged girls should be punished only by their mothers. Our darling has been taller and stronger than her mother for years, and it would be too weird to tie her down for her paddling. So it's my job.

I don't expect her to hold her bottom perfectly still under the paddle — obviously it's going to tremble and bounce around — but she knows not to twist away or try to protect herself with her hands. If she dislikes a spanking, she dislikes a second spanking a day later even more for not taking it well.

I always spank Laurie on the bare bottom. That's how my wife did it when our daughter was younger. When Laurie reached her teens, and I took over parental spanking duties, I wanted to let her wear panties or a bikini, but my wife overruled me and now I know she was right. To let Laurie cover herself seems to me a sort of teasing and false modesty that is sexually suggestive and unhealthy. Much better to use the natural approach.

We don't make a big deal out of it. I don't strip her. She doesn't have to strip in front of me. She gets over my lap. I lift her skirt or pull down her pants. Then I pull her panties down just far enough to completely bare the buttocks down to the thigh crease. I have a perfect view of the sit spots and the panties partly block my view of her girl parts. Bent over my knee like that, I do see her anal button while I'm spanking her, especially if she kicks her legs in pain, but that can't be helped. If she finds it embarrassing (she does!) it's just part of the punishment along with the pain and she should behave better.

Laurie does feel her spanking acutely. I spank her a dozen times with my hand only, merely as a warmup. Then she gets the rest with a large flat hairbrush that perfectly fits her bottom cheeks. I spank first one side, then the other, warming the "sit spots" on both cheeks and especially burnishing the bottom/thigh areas. I take a long time between spanks so she feels the full effect of each smack and the punishment is prolonged. I give a good wrist snap at impact, and the hairbrush makes a loud popping sound. If I haven't hit cleanly, it makes a thud, but I am almost perfect after years of experience.

Laurie tries to be a brave girl but always ends up crying most of the way and for minutes afterward. She doesn't plead anymore, knowing it does no good. Her tears and pleas would soften me toward Daddy's Girl. But my wife is made of harder metal, and is usually the one who makes sure the spanking continues well after I'm ready to stop. She judges by color, heat, tears and body trembling.

After the spanking, Laurie is put in the corner for five minutes, standing with her burnt bottom on display. She finds that childish position embarrassing, too, but standing straight with her legs together, she doesn't show much. Unlike some of your other readers, she is allowed to rub her bottom. It doesn't make the pain go away.

Laurie says she hates being paddled, especially by her daddy and over the knee and bare. She says the pain is awful and it isn't right for us to embarrass her like this. But the proof that she hates being spanked is that she really *does* try to be good, because she really *doesn't* want to be spanked. I'm proud of my wonderful daughter. I'm also proud that I haven't let my natural tendency to baby her stand in the way of what's necessary for her good. (Of course, my wife is usually there to make sure I do a good job!)

When I took over paddling duties when Laurie reached her teens, she used to say we should discuss punishment with her and she should have a choice. At first my wife would reply, "You made your choice when you [drove too fast, smoked, talked back to your teacher, forgot your chores twice in one week, rode on a motorcycle with Robby, etc.]."

Then one day my wife got tired of Laurie's whining about choice. So she offered Laurie a choice:

"I understand you find the spankings painful and embarrassing. If you prefer, we can wash your mouth out with soap — I mean really thoroughly, so it cakes on your gum line and you taste it for a day. Or we can give you a nice big soapy enema. Or I can ground you for four days. That would be a shame — you'd miss the dance Friday."

Laurie's only had her mouth washed out a few times, when she was much younger, and she hates that. She hates enemas even more. And she hates being grounded even more than that.

So it's been spankings ever since. If she protests, my wife reminds her she has a choice.

THE TUTOR'S DUTIES

— CLAUDE D., EDINBURGH, SCOTLAND

Your publication provides a lot of eye opening information about different kinds of spanking and different reasons for spanking. I am especially intrigued by the letters from girls and women who like to be spanked, some mildly, some severely.

To me, there is a difference between spanking and cruelty or sadomasochism. Spanking is a part of sex play. Spanking alone can bring some people to climax, both spanker and spanked. Or it can get them excited, as foreplay to sex. I am sure many men spank their wives, girlfriends, daughters, servants, pupils, foster daughters or whatever on the pretense of seeking to discipline and improve them, when deep down the reason is their own sexual pleasure. They like to get a female (and sometimes, regrettably, a male) over their lap, uncover their buttocks and spank enough to cause pain, reddening and heat.

Often such men place the spanked female in such a position that she shows her charms as well as her buttocks, and the men feel the buttocks frequently to judge the effect of the spanking. This may all be painful for the spanked female, and embarrassing as well, but I wouldn't call it sadism unless it reaches the point of cuts, bruises, o color that stays more than a day. It is just sexual play, whether or not the spanker cares to admit the fact to himself. And often the spanker's pleasure is mirrored by the spankee's, whether she admits it to herself.

I had occasion to think about all this when I worked one summer at a luxurious villa on a lake near the Switzerland–Italy border. I was a tutor and part–time male governess for two girls, aged 14 and 16, and their brother, aged 15.

I noticed immediately that the younger daughter would do things to provoke her father to spank her. She'd interrupt him when he was speaking with me, she'd use bad words, she'd tease her brother, or her father would ask her to do something and she'd say, "Later, Poppa."

He'd warn her once or twice, "Maria, you're headed for a spanking," and then she'd repeat the conduct. She'd keep acting the brat until he gave up and tossed her over his knee. Then he'd lift her skirt out of the way, pull down her panties to her knees, and spank her. It was only with his hand, he never blistered her with a shoe or hairbrush or anything, but his hand was strong enough and he was thorough.

If Marie's brother and sister were around, they'd watch the spanking. If I was around, I'd be asked to watch. Her father, ever a gentleman, would make sure I had a good view right behind her buttocks, before baring and spanking his daughter.

Marie would blush and carry on, yelling "No, not my panties! Not in front of him!" (meaning me). She'd yell for her mother to save her, which was absurd, since her conduct annoyed her mother even more than her father. She'd kick, cry, complain and plead for mercy during the spanking, but her father would keep it up till the two very cute white cheeks would turn an even cuter bright red. If there's anything prettier than a teenage girl's buttocks, it's her buttocks after being spanked.

This was the first time I'd ever seen a spanking. (I was 21 and must have led a sheltered life!) I'd never been spanked and never spanked anyone, even a girlfriend in play. But watching these spankings of Marie, I wondered if I'd get the chance to try my hand.

That happened sooner than I expected. After Marie's second spanking, her father invited me out to the patio for a cigar and brandy. He said the girls' doctor had told him the best medicine for a teenage girl is a thorough spanking on her nude behind. He said this was good for her complexion and maturing sexual organs, helped prevent monthly cramps, and was the best punishment for naughtiness, so it served many purposes. He also said it got rid of physical modesty.

The doctor emphasized the girl's buttocks should be nude for the spanking. He said the nudity helped young women become more comfortable with their bodies.

Then the surprise. The father gave me authority to spank his children. I had gained his trust and I had his blessing to stand in for him and his wife, especially since he was often away on business.

Marie tested my patience a few times, each time stopping her misbehavior when I warned her. Then she went far enough, and I got the chance to do what I had only watched. Seeing her buttocks redden under her father's hand was one thing, but getting her body over my lap, pulling her panties down and spanking her was special. Interestingly, her brother and sister didn't intercede for mercy; they encouraged me.

"Do a good job, like Poppa does," said her sister. "He's going to ask us how you did when he gets back." So I spanked Marie long and hard. I had no experience but got the hang of it soon enough. She kicked, bawled and begged just like she had with her father, but I still spanked her till her cheeks were bright red and hot to the touch, which I checked frequently. Her brother said, "Check with your hand and see if she's getting hot."

In fact, her brother and sister enjoyed the whole show immensely. Their sister was going through a brat stage and they were happy to see her comeuppance. They didn't gloat but, as I said, encouraged me to do a "complete job."

When I finished spanking Marie, I put her on a hard stool in the corner for thirty minutes. That hurt her heated buttocks and the boredom was a punishment in itself. I didn't think her father would mind that either, and he didn't. When he returned home that evening, he inspected Marie with approval and told me, "She's still red. Nice job. If your hand hurts, you're welcome to use her hairbrush or table tennis bat."

After that spanking broke the ice, spanking was the order of the day for all three children. Truth to tell, the other two were much better behaved, and each was over my lap only twice during the summer. I'm sure spankings were nothing but pain and embarrassment to them. Marie's older sister was, if anything, even prettier than her sister, and seemed to feel the punishment more acutely. I enjoyed spanking her as much as I did Marie. The boy took his punishments like a man. I neither liked nor disliked spanking him.

But Marie, being incorrigible, was over my knee at least once a week, and often over her father's knee as well. I am positive that, despite the pain, she got sexual gratification out of the spankings. I think the embarrassment of being bared also got her oddly excited. If she didn't enjoy the spankings, she would have avoided rather than provoked them. Her father said their doctor quoted Freud: said, "All women are exhibitionists at heart, especially when they're adolescents."

As for me, unlike some of your other readers, I won't pretend I didn't enjoy putting Marie's warm body over my knee for a nice session with my hand, and now and then the hairbrush. I would get terribly excited during the spanking and shortly afterward would retire to my room to relieve myself. I didn't tell her parents she got excited during her punishment. And she didn't tell on me.

Aside from Marie's brattiness which drove her brother and sister crazy, the three children were delightful and got along well. Interestingly, they were quite comfortable with nudity around each other. There was a swimming pool, and often the children wouldn't bother with bathing suits if there were no adults around. (A lot of their friends were similarly casual.) The villa featured gigantic bathrooms with huge sunken tubs; the three thought nothing of sharing the tub as they had when they were much younger, scrubbing each other's backs.

I believe Marie's spankings did her good. She had a perfect complexion, much better than most girls her age, and she ended her brat stage shortly after my employment ended. I hope the spankings had something to do with it.

I have employed spanking with several of my girlfriends since that summer (others wouldn't hear of it) and it's done my present girlfriend a lot of good. I wish I could show you how attentive she is now and how much happier as well. If I say, "Lisa, please bring me coffee," it's in my hand in seconds. If I say, "Lisa, please bring a stick of butter," she knows we're going to play train and tunnel. If she delays, she knows she'll go over my knee until her bare bottom is hot to the touch. And if that doesn't do the trick, over the couch arm or bent over the footstool for a few well–aimed strokes with my belt.

I am very grateful to my employer that summer for giving me such an enjoyable experience in raising and punishing children. (Unfortunately I never got to meet the children's doctor with all the interesting ideas.) Like I say, I am honest with myself. I am honest in saying that Marie enjoyed her spankings and they did her good. I am honest in saying her brother and sister cordially hated being spanked. I am honest in admitting I got great pleasure in spanking Marie and her sister. I see nothing wrong in personally enjoying punishing the girls when they had earned punishment and it was good for them anyhow. I enjoy spanking my present girlfriend and she must get something out of being spanked or she'd leave.

Despite the pain of being spanked, I've never injured any girl or woman. They're good as new within hours or at worst a day. A girl's buttocks, or a woman's, are designed to feel pain but with plenty of protective padding.

[Editor's Note: This letter illustrates the continuing discussion about the proper role of spanking. To what extent is spanking an erotic activity? To what extent is it a disciplinary activity? To what extent is it both? Is it appropriate for the spanker to erotically enjoy administering a spanking if the spankee isn't enjoying the spanking at all? Is it true that many disciplinary spankings are really for erotic pleasure — either of the spanker who looks for chances to spank, or of the spankee who provokes a spanking, or both in an unspoken "dance?" To what extent do people admit such motivations,

rather than bury them in their subconscious?
Or should we just conclude that spanking has so many meanings, conscious and unconscious, varying with person and relationship, that it means something different to each person and it is impossible to fit the activity into simple categories?]

x x x

THROWN OVER A LOG, SWITCHED AND TAKEN DOGGIE–STYLE

— MAE O., WEST VIRGINIA

[This is taken from a much longer letter which includes many non–spanking activities. By the way, "ridge runner" is a polite term for "hillbilly, a derogatory word for natives of the Appalachian Mountains .]

I arrived at his house late, and nervous because I know tardiness means extra punishment. I was promptly ordered into position for a paddling. I waited on the bed on all fours, with my dress hiked up above my waist and clipped to my blouse, and my bottom up in the air. After five minutes he was back, feeling my bottom through my panties, then tucking them into my butt crack. Then he paddled away with his Spencer paddle, the kind with two rows of holes drilled in it. The holes supposedly help it go faster through the air by reducing wind resistence and increase the smart by getting rid of any air cushion between the paddle and my pert, girlish buttocks. At least that's how men describe them. His paddle hurts like dickens, but all paddles do. They say the holes can cause blisters but he knows all the tricks and I've never had that problem. Not that I'd mind seeing how it felt once, anyhow.

While he paddled me, he lectured me about my errors. At one point I thought to myself, "God! How can I take any more?" That was when he told me the regular paddling was over, and the next five were for the tardiness. All of those were right on the old sit spot, and I thought I'd faint. He let me get off hands and knees and lie down on the bed while he massaged my back. It was strange to feel his wonderful hands on my back, and then massaging my pussy lips and then parting them and in my sex, while my poor behind continued to burn.

A few minutes later, after my apologies for my errors and tardiness, I was forgiven and we were on the road.

Through the trip, my bottom ached and throbbed, as I kept shifting and trying to sit sideways. It reminded me of coming pleasures at some convenient motel. We stopped at 10:00 p.m. and got a deal on a room. When you show up that late, you can always get a deal. The office reeked of curry but our unit was terrific, spic–and–span with a big shower and tub. My tardiness was forgiven by now and we made love, interspersed with hand slaps. When you've already been paddled, it doesn't take much of a slap to make you feel it.

Upon arrival at the event the next morning, we were greeted by our friends and enjoyed barbeque and cold drinks, with bluegrass music playing from a boom box. I was in ridge runner heaven. But eventually he caught my eye and gave me That Look, and we sneaked out through the trees that surrounded the house. We were delighted to see — hickory trees. A confirmed spanker knows what trees produce the best switches.

It has always been my job to fetch the instrument of my punishment. He told me what to look for, and I waded through the tall weeds, getting scratches and itches on my legs and hoping I wasn't picking up ticks and who knows what. I chose three branches. There were many, but those spoke to me. Like looking at a row of rattan canes and somehow lighting on one and somehow knowing deep down, "That's the one."

I knew he intended to switch me right there and then. We were still close to the party; we could hear the music and laughter. I hoped no one would blunder onto us.

You may be surprised to know I'd never been switched. I'd never even seen anyone switched, although some of my friends growing up got it regularly and would show me the aftermath — cute teenage girl buttocks laced with thin pink lines. I'd never cut a switch or prepared one. But I'd read about them and knew what to do. The knobs and irregularities had to be cleaned off. So I did what I could with my trusty sheath knife. All ridge runners carry one.

He inspected all three branches, chose one and kept two in reserve.

Then, with me still nervous about wandering partygoers who might blunder onto us when they decided to go off into the woods for hanky panky, I "dropped 'em" and bent myself over a fallen log. I heard the words "raise up an inch," then felt his hands yanking my panties to my knees. I could feel a breeze on my bare behind. Then he was squeezing and kneading my cheeks.

Then I got the switch for the first time in my life, and found out what all the excitement was about and why it's such a country favorite.

I heard a hum in the air and a moment later my very first stroke of a switch. He gave me four or five hard whacks with his freshly made mini–whip. Good grief! Yow! Super ouch! The switch really really *really* stung. First a super sharp pain, then a nasty burn that went on and on. Lying over the log like that, I could hardly move or shift my weight. I didn't *dare* get up. I didn't dare put my hands behind me, even for a moment. There was no way to get rid of the shooting burn of that thin, whippy weapon. All I could do was try to get my breath back and anticipate the next painful stroke.

He said he gave me sixteen strokes. "Took it easy on you because you're a beginner," he added. It felt like eleventy eight gazillion strokes. But when I looked at myself in the mirror later, I counted only sixteen lines. Still visible and still painful.

Then, of course, with me bent over the log in perfect position and still shuddering, he couldn't resist my perfect body. He took me hard from behind, and it was incredible. Then I felt the greasiness of lubricant *there* — he'd thoughtfully brought a tube — and he took me in my behind, pinning me to the log. It was uncomfortable at first, as usual, but I managed, as I had to, and got into it. There's nothing like being thrown over a log, having your clothes pulled down, getting switched half to death, getting fucked doggy style and getting taken in the ass, all while you're afraid your friends will blunder on the scene. Having the party so close did discourage me from yelling, though.

Then darned if I didn't get another few with the switch and I felt like I'd sat on a stove.

Then we rejoined the party, the evidence all hidden under my jeans, and no one the wiser. But I was wincing with each step in those tight jeans, and I got a knowing smile or two.

x x x

MY SPANKING PUNISHMENT AS A TEEN

— JOHANNA L., MEDINA, OHIO

With school being out for the summer, half my kids' friends under the age of sixteen seem to be grounded half the time for one thing or another. Not getting home on time, having tobacco on their breath, forgetting errands and chores, playing video games in their pajamas all day. It got me thinking about how things were dealt with by my parents back in the Old Days.

Naturally, since I am writing to you, my reveries turned to spanking. And the role that it plays in family life (and education too, back then). And the dramas which revolved around spanking. If Shakespeare said "all the world's a stage, and we but players," then plenty of family dramas revolve around spanking. Suspense, crime and punishment, judges and juries, trials, nudity, voyeurism, pain, uproar, and sexual excitement, all mixed in together. And everyone in the family was a player, one way or another.

So let's talk about these dramas at my house back when I was 15 and 16, in the budding flower of my womanhood, y and beautiful. I had a younger sister and brother, twins, 14 and darlings. When they were kids and wore their hair the same, you'd have to look closely to tell them apart. But back to the mini–plays at my house. They were great, as long as my brother or sister was the lead, not me. When I was the feature, I didn't appreciate my starring role and would have preferred not to have an audience.

There were certain spankable offenses and all of us knew the rules. The worst offense was talking back, especially to our mother. Another biggie was taking His name in vain, sort of like talking back to God. Another major offense was lying, especially to our parents, but lying to teachers and other adults counted too. There were other, more minor offenses which might or might not result in a spanking. So we had the drama of not knowing whether there would be a happy or unhappy ending.

Back to lying, though. A blatant, outrageous, knowing whopper was one thing. There was no getting around it and no way to plead for leniency. There was only the elegant point–counterpoint of crime and punishment with the resolution consisting of a mortified, red–buttocked crying adolescent.

But there were sometimes shades of untruth, also. Like, "I didn't know what time it was," which could also mean "I was having too much fun to bother checking the time." There was some wiggle room, and getting home late wasn't a mortal offense. One could get addicted to using stretchers.

Once I got out of punishment by showing my parents my watch had lost half an hour and misled me. "How can I be blamed when the watch *you* bought me lied to me?" I pled. They never knew I set the time back when I realized I'd be home 45 minutes late from a making–out session.

When dad got home from work, the stage would be set. First off, there was silence on the set. Dad worked in a machine shop. The machines made a racket and employees had to shout over them. As a result, dad loved peace and quiet. When he walked in the door, the radio went off, record players went off and the TV went off. Everything was off for 45 minutes.

Really, silence is a blessing. Dad needed some peace and quiet and honestly, so did we. We could read and do our homework. Meanwhile dad would get out of his dirty work clothes, shower, take a 15–minute cat nap and put on comfortable clothes and slippers. Mom would wake him up and we'd all sit down to dinner.

All the events of the day were reviewed at the dinner table, even the spankable ones. But those were only touched upon; the real review and discussion didn't come till later. The dinner table was a place for harmony, discussion and wit, not discord. It wasn't the place to resolve crime and punishment.

The place for that was in front of the judge's bench — dad's giant easy chair. And that came after dinner, after the children left the table and he and my mother had talked, and after he finished skimming the evening paper.

You'd have an hour after your behavior got mentioned at dinner, to think about the looming threat of punishment and how you might fend it off. Meanwhile you'd do the dishes or take out the garbage, or whatever you thought might get mom and dad in a more charitable mood.

Usually by the hour of your trial, you'd figured out the arguments you were going to make, or your plea for mitigation. Still, you'd worked yourself into a state. Meanwhile the siblings would have given you advice if they were in a good mood, or teased you if they were feeling mischievous. All just lead–up.

Then came The Lecture. You had to stand — literally — before the judge and listen to every word and answer every question. It took forever. He could say more than any man about, say, coming home on time or the risks of driving too fast. And he spoke slowly. English was his second language. He was fluent in it but for deep thoughts he had to think in Danish and translate.

It was a struggle to pay attention and act like I was listening. If he caught me napping on my feet, he'd say, "Maybe I wasn't clear," and start over. Having to listen to the lecture from the bench exhausted the body and numbed the mind. There went half an hour, but it felt like an hour and a half. Time drags when you're bored. But you had to stay awake because at the end you'd have your chance to try to argue your way out, or at least plead for mercy.

During all this, the other children might be present, enjoying the accused's discomfort and secretly betting with each other what the punishment would be. Or they might value their time and come in only when dad was ready to pronounce verdict and sentence.

Dad was reasonable. I'll grant him that. He would as soon spare us punishment. He wasn't one of those parents who say "this hurts me more than it does you," while enjoying punishing you. We might escape with extra chores instead of a spanking.

Only after all this high drama did we get to the spanking. As with all that came before, it was a ritual, a script if you please, though with room for ad libbing you might say.

Once judgment was pronounced — there was no appeal from this court — the family played their supporting roles. Our mother hated to see us spanked, so she would go off to the kitchen or her sewing. The twins would grin at each other and find good spots for viewing. And I — well, what could I do but follow instructions and help my dad with my final humiliation?

"Fetch the Chair," dad would tell me. Obediently, I would fetch it. The chair was a sturdy armless hard backed thing from the old country. I also fetched a big pillow for the chair.

"Put it where it belongs," he'd say. I did.

"No, turn it the right way," he'd say. (I'd put it where my sibs could only see the spanking from the side.)

I'd face it the right way.

"Fetch The Strap." I ran to do that too. Didn't dare not to. There I was, fetching all the instruments of my own ordeal for the judge, jury and executioner. Even condemned men aren't asked to tie the noose around their own neck.

Then the ultimate.

"Take everything off."

I didn't dare hesitate with that either. Off came my skirt. Off came my panties. When dad said "off," he didn't mean "pull them down," he meant "take them off." I couldn't take my clothes to my room, there was no place to hang them in the living room, and I couldn't toss them onto the couch. I had to hand them to my grinning brother and sister. If my shirt was too long and fell onto my buttocks, dad would have one of the twins pin it up with a clothespin.

So the stage was almost set, with the lead standing there nude below the waist in front of dad and the grinning twin imps. Well, not *quite* the worst. One time, my sister had hesitated to take her panties off, so dad made her take *everything* off. Shirt and bra as well as panties. She got her spanking *completely* nude. So when dad told us to bare ourselves, we hustled to clear our buttocks.

"I'm sorry it's necessary to punish you," dad would say. "Place yourself in position."

That meant over the chair, with my hips resting on the pillow for comfort and, more importantly, to raise my buttocks up. My legs would dangle on one side, barely touching the floor, and my head and arms would hang down on the other. The floor was oak but there was a Persian carpet where The Chair was placed. Deep red with some yellow; I can almost sketch the pattern from memory. The carpet had an aroma — of fiber? Wool? Dye? If someone blindfolded me and held a patch of it in front of my nose today, my mind would go back to the spankings.

"Move your legs apart," dad would say. He thought it gave me better support. I thought it showed the twins everything. It wasn't the first time they'd seen me, but this was nudity mixed with *humiliation and punishment*. That's different.

But I digress. I'd place myself in position. Dad would say again he was sorry he had to punish me.

Then, whack! Whack! Whack! As many times as I was punished, I never got used to the pain, never found a way to get ready for it or make it less. Each smack was a shock, an agonizing jolt that went right into the muscle and radiated up and down and then burned and throbbed terribly. And after a pause it was followed by another even worse. I didn't dare yell or scream; didn't I mention dad worked in a loud shop and loved peace and quiet? I screamed once but it didn't end my spanking; instead it got me extras.

After three, there'd be a pause, then whack! Whack! Whack! Even worse, landing on already burning flesh and with dad all warmed up.

Another pause, then whack! Whack! Whack! I'd think I couldn't take even being touched. I'd want to kick my legs, but in that position it's hard to. It puts all the pressure on the hips and makes you feel like you might topple out of position. I kicked hard one time — *I couldn't help it* — and nearly fell off the chair. Dad gave me two extra swats. I didn't do that any more.

Then I'd get my final three. Whack! Whack! Whack! By that

time, I'd be crying hard, my tears pouring onto the beautiful carpet, my face contorted from pain and reddened from shame and that face down posture, my body shaking, my breath coming in gasps.

My sister told me once, "Your butt made little twitches after the spanking like it was having a spaz attack." Very funny. Kids say the darndest things, don't they?

Dad would say to my sibs, "Take a close look so this can be a lesson to you two also." And they'd come take a close look at my scalded, shaking, *open* buttocks. They'd make comments like, "Gosh, sis, does it hurt much?"

Assuming I'd behaved, that was the end. Dad would have the twins help me up and support me for a minute in case I got dizzy. The last thing he'd tell me was, "I'm sorry I had to punish you. Put everything away."

The last thing I'd say was, "Thank you, Daddy." ("For what?" I'd say to myself.)

Still bare, I had to put the chair back where it came from. I had to wash off the strap with special leather soap to keep it soft and flexible, and hang it to dry. Only then was I was allowed to demand my clothes from the twins, who'd been enjoying watching me clean the tool of my punishment.

Then I'd go off to my bedroom and lie there on my side or tummy, wishing the pain would go away. The curtain had fallen on the final act. Everyone had played their parts to perfection. The play, such an audience favorite, had been played once again. Dad had starred, I had starred, and the twins had played their cameos and served as the audience too.

And soon enough, I'd have forgotten my lessons and there would be a repeat performance. Though sometimes my sister or brother would play the starring role, and I would play a cameo and serve as the audience. And much as I loved those two, I always got a thrill out of seeing *their* cute bodies over the chair, and *their* cute buttocks bouncing and turning hot and angry red under the strap. A few times they got in trouble together, and my cup overflowed, if I'm not mixing metaphors. The first time that happened, they complained about dad punishing them together. He said if they didn't like him punishing them together, he would have *me* punish them together. That gained their eager cooperation at once, unfortunately. I would have found it interesting.

Those strappings were memorable dramas. They were painful and embarrassing at the time, but I didn't resent them. I never got a strapping I didn't deserve, and I escaped some I did deserve. The same is true of the twins. By the way, although we enjoyed each other's strappings, we didn't gloat afterward and we never told our friends on each other.

I don't think dad's punishments warped any of us emotionally. They didn't turn us into sadists and masochists. As an adult I've never sought to whip anyone or get myself whipped. I'm married and my husband and I don't strap each other. The most we've done is half–serious birthday spankings in private. The twins are both married now. We talk about everything and I know neither of them is into corporal punishment. None of us spank our kids or plan to. We all see our parents often and have never asked dad for a strapping for old times' sake.

x x x

DISCIPLINE FROM DAD; EROTIC SPANKINGS FROM HUBBY

— JANE B., MILWAUKEE, WISCONSIN

I don't think a spanking is *either* punitive or sexual. It can be either or both. It depends on the individual relationship and circumstances.

I'm in my mid–twenties and live in a large Midwestern city. Since my mid teens I have had long term spanking relationships with three men, and one night stand and short term relationships with dozens. My emotions have been completely different at different times, even with identical spankings from the same guy. By the way, I go for a particular physical type: medium height, dark hair and eyes, reasonably good looking and fit.

Each time the spanker has prepared me himself by firmly taking my arm, pulling me to him, putting me across his knees after first seating himself in a straight armless chair, and clearing any clothing from my waist to my knees, leaving me bare. He has then spanked my bare tush hard with his hand from two dozen to four dozen times. I end up with my nether cheeks bright red and covered in hand prints. I have discoloration and marks for two days and sitting is miserable for at least a day.

The first of these men was — of course! — my daddy, who took over discipline chores from my mother when I grew bigger and stronger than her at age 14. Daddy was a loving but very stern and upright man, and I assure you that sexual feelings to-ward his daughter or any pleasure in my nudity or pain were the farthest thing from that good man's mind. Sexual feelings were the farthest thing from my mind, too, and there was no pleasure for me, only pain and embarrassment. And unlike some of your readers who talk about getting sexually excited by forced nudity and embarrassment, I had no sexual feelings at all.

My father's attitude was that since I had done something wrong, spanking me and making me suffer would help me re-member not to do it again. One time, as he was getting ready, he said, "If I can't get the lesson into your head, maybe I can get it into your buttocks."

I did suffer from these painful spankings, terribly. I also hated my mother and father seeing my private parts nude. Although my mother didn't spank me, she would watch. "We're in this to-gether," they'd tell me. My father wouldn't stop spanking me un-til my tush had reached the proper shade and my attitude had reached the proper stage of repentance. My mother decided when the spanking was done and signaled my father. By that time I was a limp, crying, repentant young lady.

After the spanking my parents would hug me and tell me how much they loved me. I think that's valuable. After a spanking a girl needs reassurance of her parents' love. Those lessons did sink in and four or five lessons each year by way of my buttocks were enough to keep me straight.

My parents didn't use other methods like grounding, for which I was grateful. My friends who got grounded wished their parents would spank them instead. My friends who got spanked preferred spanking to grounding unless the spankings were truly brutal.

Spanking was an accepted means of parental discipline where I grew up. One time I had to go to the doctor (not for the spanking, just for a checkup). When the nurse turned me over on the table it was obvious I'd been spanked, but all she said was, "Looks like a young lady has been naughty." Similarly, at school in the P.E. locker room girls would show up with blushing tushes. No one ever thought to call the police and make a federal case out of it.

My second experience with spanking was with a young advertising agency owner for whom I worked. In my late teens, going through a belated rebellious phase, I went in for purple streaks in my hair, skirts that were too short, blouses that were too low-cut and heels that were too high. My boss was young and unmarried and we had a comfortable and rather informal work relationship. Several times he questioned my choice of clothing. Finally he said maybe he needed to spank me the next time I dressed "unprofessionally."

I had a funny feeling when I heard that. Of course it tickled my curiosity and after thinking it over I came in dressed "unprofessionally" again. He raised his eyebrows but said nothing till closing time except to ask me to stay late. When everyone else had gone he locked the office door and grabbed me. I expected a few love taps over my skirt, but it came down quickly, then, despite my protests, so did my panties. I got two dozen hard whacks, like my father used to give me. I'm sure dad would have approved.

However, I could hear my boss laughing as he spanked me. When I twisted around I could see him grinning as he restrained me and spanked away. Although the spanking hurt and tears came by the end, I enjoyed the experience too.

After that, I chose more normal clothing and hair grooming. My boss was a great guy and I did want to make a good impression with clients on his behalf. But about once every two weeks I'd get the itch and give him an excuse to put me over his knee again.

I know he enjoyed spanking me. He'd draw out the punishment, squeezing my bottom cheeks between spanks and telling me how red I was. I got a thrill out of those spankings too. I loved them even when he provided himself with a ping pong paddle. That ratcheted up the pain a lot, but I still enjoyed it.

Although I got a thrill out of him controlling me and seeing my parts, we never went any farther with each other because he had a steady relationship. I would have been more than willing.

My third spanking relationship, and the one that's plainly sexual in nature, is with my husband. When we met we knew we were interested in each other, but were reluctant to go any farther than some heavy kissing. Then I annoyed him by forgetting to do something important, and annoyed him again when he showed up that evening to pick me up for a play and found I had hardly started to dress. Meaning we'd probably miss the first act.

He said something about promptness and reliability and being considerate, I said something in return, he threatened to "blister your butt till you'll have to watch the play standing up," and I told him he wouldn't dare try.

I don't know whether he would have stripped me if I'd been fully dressed, but I'd just come out of the shower and had nothing on but a towel, and that came off in our argument. He took that as an invitation. He grabbed me, *sans* towel, *sans* everything except water droplets, and threw me over his lap, to my outrage.

He spanked me a few times with his hand and asked whether I'd learned my lesson. I said "no" and kept struggling. Then he reached for my hairbrush and laid into me. He paddled away till my rear shined like the setting sun and I was sobbing and yelling "I've learned my lesson, I've learned my lesson."

When he let me up his manner had changed and he was so excited he was breathing hoarsely. He kissed me hard, had his hands all over my breasts, and moments later threw me back on the bed and got rid of his suit. He took me right there, and after a few minutes took me again. He told me I had the world's greatest body and the world's prettiest bottom, and spanking improved it. We were in love after that if we weren't already, and married as soon as we decently could. We never did make it to the play, so I don't know how *Our Town* came out in the end!

Although my husband is a gentle soul, our best lovemaking happens after I tease him into spanking me. He gets excited when he realizes a spanking is in the offing, and I get excited when I'm over his lap feeling my bottom globes shining with heat and pain that radiates to my pussy. And I find ways to rub myself on his knees while he's spanking me. After the spanking we always have sex. We even have anal sex sometimes. Normally I'm not crazy about that but I get so excited by being spanked I'll allow anything, and my sexual "heat" seems to make it easier for me to take him in my butt.

My husband and I don't do "disciplinary" spankings. Our spankings are blatantly erotic. They are foreplay or almost sex acts in themselves, and we both know it. We limit ourselves to his hand and two handy hairbrushes which we keep within reach of our bed. We've tried things like a belt, paddle, strap and cane, but didn't stay with them. First, they hurt too much; I want spankings, not beatings. Second, with me bent over and him swinging from distance, they lack the intimacy of the over the knee position, where we feel the warmth of each other's bodies, I feel securely held, and he can continually feel my buttocks or use his fingers in my sex.

So, though spankings may be almost identical, they reflect different relationships and feelings. With my father, there was that special father–daughter bond and the spankings were 100% disciplinary. With my boss, a superior–subordinate relationship mixed with friendship and unresolved sexual tension. With my husband, an intimate bond and spankings that are totally erotic for both of us.

Or, I wondered, did my different feelings merely show my own erotic blossoming? Had my body been trained over the years to respond to spanking? Then, a few months ago, my husband was away for several months outside the country, and I visited my parents for several weeks. While there I said something that upset my mother very much. Although I pleaded that I was a grown woman and no longer under their authority, my father put me over his knee for a spanking.

The procedure was just the same as when I was a teenage girl. My panties came down first. Then I got an even worse spanking than when I was younger. Dad and mom must have decided since I was older and bigger I could take a worse blistering. So after what seemed like dozens of spanks from dad's hands, mom handed him her hairbrush and he spanked me with that about a jillion times.

My poor behind hurt worse than ever, and I cried and sobbed and apologized. I assure you I had no erotic feeling at all from this miserable experience. Not from being stripped by "a man in authority. Not from being embarrassed by my nudity in front of him and my mom. Not from the paddling itself or the pain, and there was plenty of pain. Not even from my privates rubbing on his knees as I bounced and squirmed under all those spanks. I had nothing but more of the same pain I remember from my teens. No pleasure at all.

✗✗✗

"WEIRD EXCITEMENT" FROM SEEING A SPANKING

— CARL F., SHREVEPORT, LOUISIANA

I had thought that my feelings about corporal punishment were unusual, even sick. It's a relief to find so many men and women with the same feelings and know I'm not alone.

I am in my forties, college educated and in a secure, well paid white collar job. Several years ago I married a divorcee with two very bright, very pretty, and sometimes very high spirited teenage daughters. (Her ex lived in a distant state, was ill and played no role in the girls' lives.)

Soon after our marriage, Ellen commented that her girls had been getting away with too much and were going to have to be reined in. I said they seemed well behaved to me. She said she knew them better than I did and they were getting too big for their britches. I said it was her decision how to handle them but I would back her up, whatever she decided. I joked, "What are you going to do, tan them?"

Then, in the most matter–of–fact way, she said that, indeed, they benefitted from an occasional tanning. This surprised me and bothered me too, since the girls were 14 and 16, the older one fully developed, the younger one almost so. I said they seemed a little old for her to be spanking them.

Ellen said that "old fashioned discipline" had always been

used with her daughters. And that the girls were so well behaved because of the threat of a good spanking. They weren't spanked often anymore, she said, but they knew they could be spanked instantly when they earned it.

I said I was learning all kinds of new things. However, I felt a weird excitement and the stirring of an erection from these revelations. I wondered whether I would see the girls spanked soon and wondered what it would be like. How hard? Would Ellen use just her hand or some object? Would the girls be bared for spanking? I would have pursued the matter farther but we were interrupted by other things and neither Helen nor I raised the topic again.

Two weeks later I came home from work and, seeing no one around, headed to my bedroom to change into casual clothes. On the way I heard noise coming from the room of Janet, Ellen's older daughter. Opening the door, I was surprised to find Ellen sitting on a chair with Janet draped over her lap. Janet's sun dress was pulled above her waist and her panties were almost to her knees. Ellen had her left hand firmly around Janet's waist and her right leg pinning down both of Janet's legs. With Janet jackknifed over Ellen's knee, the girl's behind was in an almost obscenely open and jutting position. I could see much more than I ever expected to.

From the hairbrush–sized red marks on Janet's bottom cheeks, I could see I had interrupted a serious spanking. Besides, Janet was crying. When she realized I was in the room, she started crying louder and begging her mother to send me away. "Please, not in front of Carl, mom. Please! Send him away!"

"I guess I'm interrupting something," I said, and started to leave, but Ellen said, "Please come in." She told her pleading daughter not to be rude to me, she wanted me to watch. Then, keeping the crying girl over her lap, she told me Janet had "gotten way too big for her britches and has earned a little spanking." Then she went back to applying the hairbrush to Janet's bottom.

Each smack made a loud noise, set Janet's target cheek to bouncing, and set off fresh tears. I was fascinated watching the hairbrush landing on one side then the other, setting fire to her reddening bottom, which quickly changed from pink to a rich hot red.

I had all kinds of emotions. I felt sorry for Janet, who was suffering shame in front of me as well as her painful punishment. But I found what was going on disturbingly erotic. I had to struggle to conceal my growing excitement.

When the punishment was over, Janet stood in front of us crying copiously. Her dress had come down again so she was decently covered, and she put both hands behind her to try to rub the pain out of her bottom.

When we left Janet's room, I wanted to talk about what happened with Ellen, but her attitude was that this was just another household chore and she had to go pick up her other daughter, then make dinner. At dinner Janet was still downcast and had trouble meeting my eye, and a shifted constantly on her seat. It was obvious what had happened, and the younger daughter, Rose, asked, "Did someone get a spanking today?"

Janet blushed but Ellen said "That's enough of that. She did get spanked and if you don't shape up it could just as easily happen to you."

After that first time, I saw other bottom–reddening sessions, always with the guilty girl over my wife's lap, bottom nude, and crying a river. Ellen sometimes used just her hand, but usually it was the hairbrush turning the bottom from creamy white to fiery crimson. When I was in the house, Ellen asked me to watch, as an additional punishment for the girl.

In my opinion spanking has obvious sexual implications. The spankings I saw excited me. I would have loved to change places with Ellen and have the girls over my own lap rather than just watch. I had fantasies about spanking Rose and Janet, one after the other, then taking Ellen over my lap, baring her and spanking her the same way she spanked her girls.

A few times Ellen suggested that I, rather than she, should administer discipline, at least when she was away. She said I could spank harder and "be more objective since I wasn't their parent." And that the girls were so shamed by me *seeing* them getting spanked that having me *do* it would make the punishment even more of a lesson.

I was very tempted but at the same time I knew I'd be treading on thin ice. I got so excited merely watching the girls being spanked that I didn't know what might happen if I did the spanking myself. Ellen would figure out it excited me. Maybe the girls would. How would they all feel then? So I said I thought it was the parent's job.

In contrast to my feelings of sexual excitement, Ellen's attitude toward spanking was matter–of–fact, commonsense and objective. Her only goal was to give a satisfactory punishment, not too much, certainly not too little. She was no more excited about it than if she'd ordered them to wash the dishes or go to bed early. For my wife, spanking has no sexual connotations at all.

It is due to her attitude that I have never disclosed to her the effect on me of seeing these spankings. I have never raised the thought of spanking her (or, if she's not willing, having her spank me) as foreplay. Does she realize the effect these spankings have on me? If she's made the connection that I'm always ready for sex when there's been a spanking earlier in the day, she hasn't said anything.

I think our case means opposite things to different individuals. For some, spanking is simply punishment and an ordinary, nonsexual part of raising children. For others, it is a powerful sexual stimulant, so strong that it can even become an obsession. There must be many people like me who hide their interest — their powerful erotic response to spanking, being spanked or even witnessing a spanking. There must be many others who are less inhibited and search out partners with like interests.

I sometimes wonder about all the school principals, teachers and gym coaches in my state who go in for paddling students in junior high and high school. Is it just a routine task for them? Or do they get sexually excited by punishing the bottoms of good looking boys and pretty girls, putting them in that submissive posture and seeing them cry? Are some of these people so interested in spanking, or in spanking young people, that it has caused them to seek a career as a school principal? I wonder sometimes.

X X X

HUSBANDLY SPANKINGS

— CAROLYN W., CHICAGO, ILLINOIS

My husband paddles me when I deserve it, and it has made me a better wife.

This started even before we were married. We were dating most evenings. One evening we had planned to go to a party given by one of our friends. At noon he called me to say there was an emergency at his office that required him to work late that evening. I was upset and gave him the silent treatment. I told him I was busy the next three nights.

Finally I realized how selfish and foolish I had been. We'd been going together a long time, we were engaged and I didn't want to lose our relationship because I'd been immature and gotten in a snit over something that wasn't his fault. So I called him and invited him over that night.

He was very nice about it, didn't act resentful or call me immature or a brat or anything. But he asked to speak to my father. (I was still living at home.) I didn't hear the whole conversation, only my father's side, but I was able to figure it out and my father filled me in on the details. My fiancé told my father that he loved me and wanted to marry me, but I'd acted up and he thought a punishment would discourage bad behavior in the future and do me good.

My father, who was of Austrian and Italian descent, had always been strict. He agreed and told my fiancé to go ahead, with

153

his blessing. "Nip her behavior in the bud," my father said.

When my fiancé arrived that evening, my father handed him a leather strap which he had used on my sister and me throughout our teens. My father invited us into the den, where he helped my fiancé tie me down across the arm of a soft chair. Then my father departed. After a short lecture, to my utter humiliation my fiancé pulled up my skirt and pulled down my panties.

I can still remember the feeling of that heavy leather strap burning my bare bottom with each stroke as my fiancé laid it on again and again. I couldn't move out of position, but I could feel my bottom jiggle with each painful strike. I cried and pleaded, but my fiancé ignored my carrying on and gave me a dose of fifteen swats before he quit. He said he had been planning to give me "my age" (18) but had mercy because I had recognized my error and hadn't resisted being punished. Meanwhile I could hear my father watching the Cubs game on television, as if leaving me to be punished this way was the most natural thing in the world.

When my fiancé got through, he didn't release me. Instead he invited my father in to see my bottom. I was humiliated all over again as they both felt the heat in my bottom and discussed the punishment. My father told my fiancé he had parental blessing for such punishment during our engagement and when we got married.

A few days later my fiancé and I discussed a number of things, including the strapping. My fiancé insisted that in our marriage he would similarly punish me if I deserved it. We would talk my behavior over frequently, and if he thought I had done anything to merit punishment, I would get the strap ("or some other suitable instrument") on my bare bottom. I didn't want to lose him, and foolishly thought my behavior would never merit a spanking, so I agreed.

When I got married, my father gave my husband a gift of a leather strap just like the one he'd used all those years. My father kept his own for use on my younger sister. I can't say I got the strap often, or that it was ever undeserved. In our first year of marriage I got strapped only seven times and every punishment was richly earned.

Originally the idea was to review my conduct once a month, on the last Thursday evening. However, my husband decided punishment was much more effective if it followed more quickly after misbehavior. So we sat down together each Thursday evening. If my behavior merited punishment, he told me so and I received it on Saturday. That gave me two days to anticipate the pain of the coming strapping.

Each punishment was given similarly to my very first, with me secured over a large easy chair and my bottom bare. Sometimes my clothes were pulled out of the way and my panties lowered. Other times I wasn't allowed a stitch. In any case this miserable position opens the bottom, adding to my humiliation, and tightens the bottom, adding to the pain of the strap.

My husband didn't invite my father over to witness me getting the strap, but once my father happened to drop in and observed my punishment. Same as the very first time, he and my husband felt my burning bottom and my father complimented my husband on doing a nice job

After the first year, I got punished less often, perhaps three or four times a year, but the punishments were always severe. My husband tied me down firmly, laid on the strap hard and long, and the pain was terrific, leaving me crying and limp. However, I still have never received an unfair punishment.

I think the strappings have made me a better wife, and I love and respect my husband for disciplining me physically, no matter how humiliating and painful the punishment. (Well, humiliation and pain is the point, isn't it?) When he weighs my behavior and tells me I have been wonderful and have done nothing to be punished for, I love him so much. And when he tells me my behavior has not been good enough and I am due to be punished, I think about my behavior and vow to improve it. Two days later he says, "Time for your little punishment, young lady." I love him so much for trying to improve me with his discipline.

My most recent punishment was only two days ago. I can still see the color when I back up to a mirror and still feel it when I sit down. We had visited friends. After too much to drink, I had said something mean about a woman who was not present. My husband hates hearing me badmouth anyone. When he caught my eye, I knew I was in for it. On our drive home I kept saying how sorry I was. He told me there was no need to discuss it again until Saturday evening.

After I was secured as usual, my husband reminded me of my behavior and the need for correction. He laid on the strap as hard as ever, but taking a long time between whacks. I'd feel the terrible impact of the strap, the shocking burn would last for a minute, then I'd have to ready myself for the next.

After I'd received fifteen smacks, my husband asked me if I'd learned my lesson. I said again and again that I had, and I'd never, ever repeat my behavior. He said he wasn't convinced, then gave me two more, to finish the worst strapping I've ever had.

My husband and I have an active and gratifying sex life. My husband's firmness in disciplining me reminds me every time of his love and caring for me. But these strappings are not part of our sex life, they are just punishment. There's nothing sexy about the punishment itself, either the anticipation, the humiliation or the pain. But getting strapped has made me a better, happier wife. If I had to do everything all over again, I would ask my husband to discipline me with the strap, even if my father hadn't suggested it.

x x x

THE OFFICE SPANKING —
"HUMILIATION, PAIN AND EXCITEMENT"

— ETHEL N., DALLAS, TEXAS

A friend of mine and I recently compared notes on a boss we'd both had (at two different times). We wonder how common our experiences are — of being spanked by our boss at work.

We had both worked as secretaries for this man, although we were called "executive assistants." My girlfriend had worked for him just before I did. She left when she got married and had to move from the area, but she helped me take her place. She never mentioned the man's ideas about discipline. She assumed she was the only one who he'd spanked. It was only by accident that we figured out he made a habit of spanking employees.

We got to talking about him because my girlfriend noticed that I was sitting gingerly and wincing. She wormed the truth out of me, then let it out that she had been subject to the same treatment.

We are sure our boss enjoyed spanking young women, but we admitted to each other we also got a strange charge out of being spanked. When we started work at that business, Mr. "Smith" explained that he was very precise about routine matters. Papers should be stapled with the staples horizontal, not vertical or slanted. We could never use a large paper clip when a small one would do. In addresses, "street" must be spelled out, not abbreviated to "St." (Really, he was obsessive–compulsive, a total fussbudget).

Mr. Smith also told us that rather than constantly nag us, be believed in immediate "correction."

Soon enough I learned what he meant by "correction." One day, hurrying to close up and escape for a date, I misfiled several important documents. Three days later, after we had both wasted hours trying to find the missing material, he realized what had happened. Mr. Smith called me into his office, locked the door and told me he intended to spank me for my "inexcusable blunder."

I was scared, confused and nervous at this announcement. I was only eighteen. I got more nervous yet tingly and excited when he pulled a small wooden paddle from his desk drawer and motioned me to come to him.

Experienced as he was, he cleared the skirt off my bottom, tossed me over his lap, adjusted me to the position he wanted, and started paddling me. That little paddle made my buttocks smart something awful as it connected again and again to the seat of my panties. I don't know how many spanks he gave me, but I would guess twelve on each buttock cheek. I cried and cried, begging him "Enough, enough!" I tearfully promised I would never make that mistake again and would pay perfect attention to my work.

I did pay closer attention to every task and after another month passed I assumed this spanking was a one time thing to get my attention. But strangely, I wanted to be spanked again.

One day I finally decided to test him. I purposely gave him some papers stapled together sloppily, with the staples cock-eyed. When he got annoyed I acted like he was being unreasonable. Soon enough I got what I wanted.

Mr. Smith grabbed me and half–walked, half–carried me to a couch. He told me to lift my skirt, and meanwhile removed his belt from his pants. This time he decided I wasn't entitled to my modesty or dignity at all. He pulled my panties down to my trembling knees and bent me over the sofa arm. "Don't even think of moving or we'll start over," he said.

I must have gotten more than twenty lashes with that dou-bled–over belt across my bare buttocks. He covered every inch, including the creases between thigh and butt. He spanked me so hard I felt dizzy. I'd never cried so much in my life.

That day I found it impossible to sit comfortably. My girl-friend and I compared notes on Mr. Smith. She told me about similar spankings she had received while working for him. As with me, he'd spanked her with his little paddle and with a belt. As with me, he had started with spanking her over panties, but later those came down too. If anything, my girlfriend got spanked far more than I had. But like me, my girlfriend found the spankings strangely exciting and she both dreaded them and looked forward to them.

We laugh about those spankings now when we get together, but at the time they were nothing to laugh about. The combi-nation of humiliation, pain and excitement awakened all kinds of new and mixed feelings in me. Those spankings were plenty painful, but still a sexual thrill. I wonder whether most young women really like to be spanked sometimes, whether or not they admit it to themselves. My girlfriend and I do.

x x x

FIRM OLDER WOMAN LAYS DOWN THE LAW

— JEFF W., YOUNGSTOWN, OHIO

I am 24 years old and married to a wonderful woman a year younger, who I will call "Jane Doe," like the courts do. My wife wanted me to tell about the following experience, and I didn't. We ended up playing head–to–head poker one evening. The stakes: the loser would have to write about a very embarrassing experience. Having been finished off with a pair of 10's that fell to her pair of queens, I am compelled to write to you, embarrassing as this experience was.

At that time we had been dating for several months. Jane was living at home with her widowed mother.

Several times I had brought my wife–to–be home very late, or rather in the wee hours. Her mother was unhappy when this happened, but I paid little attention.

One night I brought her back at 1:30 a.m. Her mother was waiting for us, and steaming. She sent Jane to her bedroom and asked me to stay for a few minutes "to discuss something." She told me she had asked me several times to bring her daughter home at a reasonable hour, not "some ungodly hour of the morning." I had paid no attention, she continued. I couldn't dispute that.

Now, she said, it was her "duty to stop this nonsense." She asked me to come to her room. That made me very nervous.

Since she obviously didn't want to make out with me, what would require such privacy? Still, I didn't want to refuse and have her keep me from seeing Jane.

She closed the door and asked me to drop my pants. Of course I said "no." So she said "You're right, they'd get wrinkled. Remove them and fold them neatly over this chair."

I still objected, so she said it was my choice, but if I didn't cooperate, she would no longer allow me to see her daughter. Jane was not yet ready to move out of her home, I didn't want conflict between her and her mother and I wanted to stay in her mother's good books. So, apprehensive and embarrassed, I removed my pants.

She moved a dresser chair into the middle of the room and armed herself with a dark wood hairbrush. She showed it to me and I got more nervous because it was large and looked heavy. She seated herself and I knew I was going to be spanked over her lap like I was a little boy, and spanked hard. I did what I could to mentally prepare myself.

She pulled me across her knees. I was assuming I'd keep my underpants on, but to my embarrassment she made me raise up so she could yank them down below my knees. I found myself in the world's most embarrassing position, a man in his twenties, bottom bared and over the knees of a firm woman about to take out her smoldering resentment on my bottom.

Then she applied that hairbrush again and again, long and hard to my bottom cheeks and the top of my thighs. She wasn't an especially strong woman, but the weight of that hairbrush and its long handle for leverage gave her hand as much power as she needed. She walloped me again and again and again.

I didn't want to break down and cry, but Mrs. Doe was intent on seeing true tears, and plenty of tears came under that endless paddling. I kept thinking surely I couldn't bear another, but every agonizing smack was followed by another, and that by another. Several times she paused, and I hoped we were done, but it was only to adjust me over her lap, stretch the fingers of her spanking hand back and forth, and then resume.

The spanking was not only painful, but I realized Jane must

be hearing me getting it. The hairbrush made a loud smack each time it landed, and I was crying as well. The shame of knowing Jane could hear the spanking was as bad as the actual pain, and that was *real* pain.

When Jane's mother finally let me up, my whole behind felt like there were hot coals on it. She made me stand in a corner, hands at my side, "no rubbing or it's back over my lap," and I felt even more like a punished little boy. She sat behind me and lectured me about respecting her and her daughter by bringing Jane home at a reasonable hour. Finally she allowed me to get dressed and go home.

It was hard to face Jane for a while after that, because, like I figured, she had heard the spanking. But she admitted something I'd been curious about; the next day, she'd gotten a thorough dose of the hairbrush to match mine. We had one more thing in common that we hadn't thought of. So I felt a little bit better. I sympathized with her. Who was I to complain over one spanking, severe as it was, when she had been spanked right through her teens and received dozens of doses of the hairbrush. (She was 19½ when this incident happened.)

After that, I was careful about getting Jane home on time, stayed in her mother's good graces and avoided any more over the knee correction. Jane and I got married six months after my spanking.

Although Jane and I sometimes give each other playful spanks with our hands during lovemaking or a more thorough spanking during foreplay, that spanking from her mother had nothing erotic about it. It was just pain and misery and embarrassing as could be.

x x x

SPANKING HIS SISTER — AND SHE LOVES IT

— NICK N., GADSDEN, ALABAMA

As a young man in his early twenties, I'd like to add my comment on one of the hot spanking topics.

A lot of fathers agonize about whether sexual feelings may arise when they spank the buttocks of their teenage daughters. Although obviously most spankings are administered by fathers, there are also others charged with the responsibility for such bare buttock punishment, such as the occasional uncle, grandfather or older brother charged with punishment duty.

In my case, I have a kid sister who is three years younger than me. When I reached fourteen my father starting giving me authority in the house when he had to travel. (My mother had passed away.) I had more and more authority and he traveled more and more in his job, knowing that I could keep an eye on things.

Among other tasks, it was my job to keep an eye on my sister's behavior and spank her when I thought she needed it. So I was fourteen and a half, but a mature and responsible, when I first put my then eleven–year–old sister over my lap for the standard punishment in our house.

Between you and me (and your other readers) there were *plenty* of sexual feelings on my part. Not at first, but when my sister started developing breasts and hips and growing a muff, *absolutely*. Are you kidding? Her perfect body over my lap, me seeing everything, her having to obey me and behave while her cheeks bounced under my hand? However, I think there were no feelings on my father's part. If she misbehaved in certain ways, she had to be spanked. If she had to be spanked, her bottom had to be bared because that's how spanking was done. But in my case, duty was definitely mixed with pleasure.

The interesting thing, however, is that judging from my experiences and observations, some girls enjoy the spanking more than the spanker does. Consider that a big, healthy teenaged girl who is determined not to be spanked presents a huge problem. The spanker is at serious risk from well–aimed feet, knees, elbows and nails. The spanker needs either enormous strength, or an extra person, or bindings, and there's still hazard along the way. I suppose the spanker can always threaten worse (mouth soaping, for example), but most do not. My dad didn't and neither did I when spanking my sister.

Yet, when such a young lady crawls meekly over her father's lap and allows him to spank her behind, then I wonder whether she must secretly enjoy her punishment despite the physical pain. Even more so when she obediently puts herself over her *brother's* lap.

With my sister, for years dad has given her a choice of punishments; a bare bottom spanking or restriction (grounding except for school or necessities like dental visits). Dad hasn't spanked me since I was 12, but up until then when I got the same choice I always chose restriction. I couldn't bear the thought of my father seeing me in that position, which was even worse than the physical pain, which I could grit my way through. I would have made the same choice through my teens and today.

But my sister . . . When she was a skinny kid, she always chose restriction. But when she started to develop, the coin flipped. She always wanted the bare bottom treatment over dad's lap. Every time. When I was in charge, she got the same choice and always wanted the spanking from me too. This was so even when the restriction would have been brief and she had nothing special planned. Which was fine with me. Monitoring a restriction is a hassle for days, while spanking her was not only enjoyable but only took only a short time and cleared the air right away.

Today, kid sister is 17, in her last year of high school. I'm 20, going to college nearby and still live at home. I am still in charge when dad is away. My sister still prefers being spanked, even severely, to even brief restriction. So, like I say, I strongly suspect she gets a sexual turn–on out of being spanked, or at least mixed feelings! And it does seem she goes out of her way to do things she knows earn punishment, and to get caught.

My dad said to me once, "You think she's starting to get funny feelings and enjoy her punishment or something?" It was awkward for him to even discuss it.

I said, "No. She just doesn't want to get cut off from her friends even for a day or two. And it's over quickly and clears the air." Etc., etc. No lawyer could have been more persuasive on the spur of the moment. Cool as a cucumber I was.

However, despite dad's suspicions and mine, I have not *seen* signs of open sexual arousal. She doesn't get wet over my knee, she doesn't try to place herself where her muff is right on my leg, she doesn't grind herself over my knee except where her body is moving with the impact of each spank, so I can't say I've proven my case. I'm sure if dad had seen anything so suspicious, the spankings would be nothing but a fond memory.

My sister is a beauty who turns heads, especially at the beach. Who can blame me for enjoying something denied to her boyfriends, when my sister has the prettiest behind in town?

I spank my sister the same way my father does. That is, her adorable bottom is cleared of jeans, skirt or shorts, followed by panties. Then she goes over my lap, where I give her as many good hard spanks as I, in my sole judgment, think she deserves. I judge when we're done by the color of her bottom, which should be bright red, the heat which I monitor by feeling her cheeks, and her crying and promises of better behavior. After the spanking, she is allowed to dress. No further lectures, standing in the corner or other punishment.

I've spoken to my sister about the spankings I give her. She says I've been fair when deciding whether she needs to be punished, she doesn't resent the spankings, she doesn't resent me for giving them, and she appreciates always being given the choice of restriction even if she always chooses spanking. She doesn't think the spankings are "too hard." She finds them embarrassing because of the nudity, even more than when dad gives them, but she realizes that's "part of the deal" so she accepts it. I have never come out and asked her if getting spanked turns her on, and she has never volunteered that information.

One other thing for what it's worth. When we were younger, we thought nothing of nudity around the house, especially on sweltering hot days. When I reached puberty, I became shyer with her. But when she reached puberty, I'd already been spanking her for two years and she was much more comfortable being nude around me, though not with her dad. She's still that way with me. She thinks nothing of asking me to come in the bathroom to scrub her back while she's bathing. Also, when she was fifteen she had a rectal problem that required daily suppositories for ten days. She could have given those to herself, but she asked me to, saying for her it was "too awkward twisting around." I didn't buy that excuse for an instant, but I was happy to perform nursing duties.

Anyhow, that's my case, why I think my sister, and lots of other women, actually enjoy being spanked. There's a lot of women being spanked, and I think many of them enjoy it. Or at least they have a lot of feelings mixed in together, and some of them are pleasant ones.

X X X

ANN LANDERS COLUMN: "A PING–PONG PADDLE KEEPS WIFE IN LINE"

— *CHICAGO SUN–TIMES, JULY 22, 1960*

The famous advice columnist Ann Landers opined now and then on topics that were considered risque for the time, including — spanking! Here she is in sanctimonious mode, impugning what sounds like consensual spanking (the information is secondhand and it's unclear whether the spanking is for discipline or enjoyment) in abusive language. Do you agree with Ann that the reasons for the spanking are "phony," since there is no evidence of "phoniness?" Do you think it's "pretty sick" to enjoy administering or receiving spankings, either for consensual discipline or pleasure? Do you agree with Ann that this is "neurotic" or worse? Do you agree that this is "sadistic" and "the line between a 'spanking' and a beating is sometimes pretty thin?" Why the sarcastic quotation marks? Did Ann fail to grasp that a "spanking" can be merely . . . a spanking? Do you think spanking during marriage shows the husband "belted her around during courtship?" Since there is no indication anyone belted anyone around during courtship, why does she assume so?

On some topics Ann Landers was rather progressive for the fifties and sixties, but on other topics it was hard to understand why anyone considered her an authority. Well, judge for yourself.

DEAR ANN LANDERS: What in the world is wrong with a husband who finds phony excuses to spank his wife at least twice a month? He keeps a ping pong paddle in the bedroom for this purpose.

The wife happens to be my sister. She told me recently this has been going on since their honeymoon last May. I never heard of such carryings on and . . . I am shocked. Is there something mentally wrong with this man?

My sister says he's a swell guy and even went so far as to defend him by admitting she usually deserves the spankings! What do you think? SIMPLY SHOCKED

DEAR SIMPLY SHOCKED: Of course there's something wrong with the man, but before you reserve a room for him in the Laughing Academy, let me suggest you make it two. Your sister is also pretty sick.

Men who enjoy inflicting physical pain on women are sadistic and the line between a "spanking" and a beating is sometimes pretty thin.

Neurotic women who feel the need to be punished seem to attract the type of man who will oblige. You say this started on their honeymoon? I'll bet he belted her around during courtship.

x x x

SPANKING IN THE NEWS

— FROM VARIOUS NEWS SOURCES

Wife Won't Take Paddling Sitting Down
— DAILY NEWS WIRE SERVICES

ROCKFORD — When Dorothy Brommerich came home too late to suit her husband, Ernest, 33, one night, he decided to teach her a lesson.

He spanked her.

Dorothy, in turn, decided to teach Ernest a lesson.

She took him to court.

Associate Circuit Court Judge Alford Penniman ruled Wednesday that the spanking constituted battery. Brommerich was fined $25.

x x x

Likes Spanking
— FROM A MARITAL ADVICE COLUMN, 1957

ANONYMOUS PRIVATE SECRETARY, THRICE EN-GAGED, AGE 29. She has had numerous pre–marital escapades with her engaged partners but all left her in a state of need after exhausting themselves. She keeps on breaking engagements, then seeking other men. "I've always been excited by dominant men; I like being spanked hard and often, made to wear form fitting tight girdles and corsets, compelled to do disagreeable tasks. Unless this is part of loving, I just don't get anything out of it at all." She cruises bars and taverns, has sought many men ... but none bothered to share her interest in spanking and this created a gap. She feels she can reach a zenith of ecstasy if a proper spanking partner could be found.

✗ ✗ ✗

Bottoms Up!
— *SEVERAL BRITISH NEWSPAPERS*

John Elliott Brooks, former mayor of Chelsen, heads for court where he's seeking a libel judgment against [a] newspaper which called him a "menace to young girls." Brooks was alleged to have advertised for "good–natured young ladies" to crew his yacht, then turned them over his knee, spanked their bare bottoms, and rubbed on whiskey "to take away the sting."

[The accompanying photograph shows a distinguished–looking older gentleman, wearing a bowler hat and carrying a folded umbrella.]

✗ ✗ ✗

Cop Fired for Spanking Two Teen Girls Who Smoked
— *ASSOCIATED PRESS*

FLEETWOOD, ENGLAND, January 24 — Constable Charles Cotton, 33, was fired from the police force today for spanking two 14–year–old girls whom he caught smoking cigarets in the street. The dismissal was announced a few hours after a local court found Cotton guilty of indecently assaulting the girls, and fined him 28 pounds.

✗ ✗ ✗

AFTERWORD

PLEASE JOIN OUR MAILING LIST

Please add your name to our Email list to receive information on future books and spanking–related news and special offers. Just visit www.SpankingBible.com and click on the link.

PLEASE SEND US YOUR SPANKING EXPERIENCE

Do you have an interesting spanking experience? We would be delighted to review it for possible publication in a future volume of this series. Just visit www.SpankingBible.com and click on the Email link.

PLEASE GIVE US YOUR COMMENTS ON THIS BOOK

We would appreciate your comments on this book. What did you like? Why? Not like? Why? Which true story was your favorite? Any suggestions for future books like this? We'd love to hear from you! Please visit www.SpankingBible.com and click on the Email link.

PLEASE POST FIVE–STAR REVIEWS AND RATINGS ON AMAZON.COM AND OTHER SITES

Please post five–star reviews and ratings on Amazon.com and other sites, so other people can enjoy this book. Thank you.

www.ingramcontent.com/pod-product-compliance
Lightning Source LLC
Chambersburg PA
CBHW051258250626
47155CB00009B/3347